THIEF OF BROKEN HEARTS

The Sons of Eliza Bryant Book One

LOUISA CORNELL

Thief of Broken Hearts: Book One The Sons of Eliza Bryant Copyright © 2018 by Pamela Bolton Holifield.

All rights reserved. No part of this publication may be reproduced, stored in a retrieval system, or transmitted, in any form or by any means without the prior written permission of the author, nor be otherwise circulated in any form of binding or cover other than that in which it is published and without a similar condition being imposed on the subsequent purchaser.

This is a work of fiction. Names, characters, places, and incidents are either the product of the author's imagination or are used fictitiously, and any resemblance to actual persons living or dead, business establishments, events, or locales, is entirely coincidental.

ISBN: 978-795714891

Cover design by Dreams2media

First Trade Paperback Printing by Scarsdale Publishing, Ltd February 2019

10 9 8 7 6 5 4 3 2

If you purchased this book without a cover, you should be aware that this book is stolen property. It was reposted as "unsold and destroyed" to the publisher, and neither the author nor the publisher has received any payment for this "stripped book."

CHAPTER 1

London
August, 1814

"Your Grace, I..."

Endymion de Waryn, Duke of Pendeen, lifted his quill mid-word. He raised his head and stared at his personal secretary... astonished. Yes. Astonished. Not surprised, as Babcock had stood there long enough to repeat those same three words twice now, punctuated by a few moments of painful silence and violent throat clearing after each utterance.

At two and thirty, Endymion had been neither astonished, nor surprised, nor shocked in nearly two decades. His carefully scheduled life precluded it, just as he preferred.

Astonished. Precisely, and the Duke of Pendeen was nothing if not precise. A quality he also expected of every man, woman, and child in his service.

"Your Grace, I..." The secretary, standing just inside the door, extended his hand. The stack of the day's post, trapped in his long, knobby fingers, fluttered like so many ivory butterflies caught in flight.

Endymion settled his writing instrument into the silver quill rest mounted on his black marble inkstand. "Babcock, I am in the room. You are in the room. I know why I am here." He cocked his head inquiringly.

"I suppose I count for nothing," a bored voice intoned from the long, silk-brocade sofa before the empty hearth across the room.

"Less than nothing. If not for the stench of your cologne, I'd have forgotten your presence entirely." Endymion shot a disparaging glance at the impeccably dressed lord draped with indolent elegance across the most comfortable piece of furniture in the room.

"I'll have you know my cologne is the finest Floris has produced in twenty years. It was mixed to my specific order." Anthony Farris, Marquess of Voil, adjusted his neckcloth and flicked a piece of lint from the top of his champagne-polished Hessians.

"You smell like a brothel on Sunday." The duke waved his secretary forward.

After a moment's hesitation, punctuated by a deep bob of his Adam's apple, Babcock minced across the Persian carpet to stand before Endymion's broad, mahogany desk. He dropped the clutch of letters onto the polished wood surface and took a step back, hands folded at the waist, one letter still in his grasp.

"How would you know? When have you ever darkened the door of a bawdyhouse?"

"I am married, Voil." A familiar twitch settled between Endymion's shoulders.

The marquess levered himself into a half-reclined position. "Not so much as anyone might notice. Least of all, your wife." He filched a lemon tart from the generous plate on the tea table next to the sofa. "I'm all for a convenient marriage, man, but, good God. Seventeen years?"

Babcock squeaked. He actually squeaked and crumpled the letter in half. Endymion leaned forward, his fingers pressed to the curved arms of his leather chair. The man took another step back.

"Stubble it, Voil. Babcock, is that letter addressed to me?" He didn't know which irritated him more—his friend's knowledge of the state of his marriage or his secretary's odd behavior.

"Your Grace, I..." The wiry man of middling years ran a finger under his neckcloth.

Endymion fixed Babcock with his most benign gaze. Having inherited his title from his grandfather at the age of twenty-five, he had a carefully practiced repertoire of expressions with which to gain the best performances from those he employed. "Well?"

"It... That is... Your Grace, I..."

"Am I paying you by the word, Babcock?"

"Of course not, Your Grace," fairly stumbled from the secretary's lips. He gasped at his own impertinence and then adopted a hushed tone. "This letter is from Cornwall, Your Grace. A second response to the invitation, that is, the letter. The letter *you* wrote. That is to say, had me to write." He swallowed hard. "*The* letter."

Endymion pushed to his feet. And immediately regretted it. Poor Babcock blanched and took yet another step back. Two more and he'd be in the corridor. At a bit over six-and-a-half feet tall, the duke tended to intimidate even when seated. Should Babcock faint, he'd never discover the problem, and he had far more pressing matters to see to today than a swooning secretary. He reached for the leather-bound volume that contained his schedules and plans for the year—each day carefully divided by the hour, tasks to be accomplished and social engagements that required his presence. He had precisely ten minutes to conclude this interruption to his afternoon.

Wait. What had Babcock said?

"*The* letter?" Scarcely out of his mouth, the question shot into his brain and bottled up the air in his lungs. He refused to look at his friend, who had suddenly unfolded himself from the sofa enough to sit up completely, too damned attentive for anyone's good. Especially Endymion's.

"Cornwall?" Voil looked from Babcock to Endymion and back. "In response to what letter? What sort of invitation?"

"One that does not include you. Aren't you expected somewhere for luncheon?" The duke stared at the single missive trapped in his secretary's shaky grip.

"By every marriage-minded mama in London. Why do you think I have sought sanctuary in the library of the dullest duke in Christendom? What letter, Babcock?" Voil had all the appearance of a hound pointing grouse.

"Don't answer that, Babcock," Endymion ordered. His secretary paled another shade and swayed slightly. To be expected of a man trapped between a marquess and a duke.

"*You* wrote to Cornwall?" Voil perched on the edge of the sofa.

"I didn't say that." A line of sweat meandered along the twitch between Endymion's shoulders. He took a casual step around the far side of his desk.

"Babcock said it." Voil pushed slowly to his feet. "You don't acknowledge the existence of Cornwall, let alone write letters to anyone there. As far as you're concerned, England stops at the River Tamar."

"Don't be ridiculous. Pendeen's family seat is in Cornwall. I am Pendeen. Therefore, I have estates to manage in Cornwall." Damn Voil for spending half his life draped over the most nap-worthy furnishings in Endymion's Grosvenor Square home.

Babcock's eyes followed this exchange, his breath bated.

Voil snorted. "Your uncle manages those estates." He sidled toward Babcock. "And writes and dispatches all your correspondence to Cornwall. Including your monthly letters to..."

The marquess's jaw went slack.

Oh hell. Endymion suppressed a groan and stepped around the front of his desk.

"You wrote to your *wife?*"

"Babcock, give me that letter." Endymion all but lunged at the terrified secretary.

Voil scrambled over a tapestry-worked ottoman and made a grab for the missive, which Babcock raised over his head, attempting to hand it off to the duke. Babcock waved his arm back and forth as the two peers shifted from side to side in an effort to capture the now much-mangled, folded, and sealed parchment. Using the three odd inches he had on his friend, Endymion snatched it from his frantic employee's trembling fingers.

He failed to resist an *"Aha!"* of triumph. Voil used that moment to snatch the letter from his hand and dance away behind the sofa.

Babcock stifled a gasp.

"Your Grace, I..." The secretary appeared torn between a bolt for the door and a bout of tears. Voil had that effect.

Endymion's reaction was far more visceral. Determined to keep his frustrated trepidation to himself, he folded his arms across his chest and leaned a hip against the desk. "Don't trouble yourself, Babcock. You and I are too far removed from our childhoods to defeat Lord Voil in such a juvenile game. His lordship is still in the midst of his."

"Says the man who has his uncle correspond with his wife on his behalf." The marquess examined the folded and sealed letter from every angle, prolonging his schoolboy antics. Endymion refused to give him the satisfaction of a reaction.

"I am accustomed to my uncle handling all of my Cornwall concerns on my behalf."

"A point on which he makes certain everyone in London is quite clear. Why he continues to do so seven years after your grandfather's death is rather less clear. To me, at least."

"Our friendship does not obligate me to offer you clarity on the management of my dukedom." Endymion might have favored Voil with one of his ducal glares, but it would have been wasted on the arrogant *arse*.

"As may be, Pendeen. However, neither you nor Babcock would be so concerned at my reading a response to one of your obsequious toad-eater of an uncle's letters. Cut line. What in God's name persuaded you to write to your wife?" He braced his hands on the back of the sofa, the letter pressed into the blue and gold brocade under his fingers.

"Uncle de Waryn has decamped to the Continent for the next few months. I had no choice." Endymion tapped a finger against the cool fabric of his jacket. A trick he'd learned long ago to clear his head when unwanted thoughts came to mind. Thoughts of Cornwall. And loss. And his wife.

Voil came around the sofa and retook his seat, the letter now dangling from his hands, which rested between his knees. "Babcock said a second response. What was the first?" Even half-asleep, the man missed nothing. Dammit.

"No."

"I beg your pardon?"

"The first response was 'no.'" Which had both intrigued and infuriated Endymion. Not that he'd give his friend that information.

"A simple 'no'? Nothing more?"

The duke and the secretary nodded in unison. Babcock cleared his throat and stared at the window at the end of the room. Plotting his escape from this debacle, no doubt. Endymion suspected he might like to join the man. Nay, he didn't suspect. He knew. The only person who wanted to read the contents of that letter more than he did was Voil. Knowledge was power. And whilst Voil knew more than anyone about Endymion's past, there were some things Endymion had kept to himself. A small bundle of power not even his grandfather had held.

"And your response to that succinct reply? Don't bother to lie about it, Pendeen. I've played chess with you for years."

"You've lost at chess with me for years." Endymion uncrossed his arms, leaned back fully against the desk, both hands gripping the ancient, polished mahogany desktop behind him. "I sent my travel carriage to fetch her. That was my response."

Voil raised a brow. He rubbed his chin with one hand, still grasping the letter in the other. "Rather like fetching an incorrigible child who's been sent down from school?"

"I would not know. I was never sent down from school." Endymion's even tone covered his inward wince. Voil's description, born of a great deal of personal experience, had struck a bit too close to the mark. Had his duchess seen it that way?

His duchess.

Voil snapped the wax seal and opened the letter. "Shall we find out how this particular child has responded to being sent for, *Your Grace?*"

Endymion pushed away from the desk but willed his feet not to move. Babcock's sharp intake of breath punctuated the silence. At least, he hoped it was Babcock's. Voil waggled his eyebrows and leaned back against the sofa cushion to read the letter.

Voil's response started with a snort. Followed by a childish chortle. In moments, Voil lay on the sofa howling with laughter. Waving that damned letter like a flag of surrender.

Endymion strode over and snatched it from the idiot's lax fingers.

"Your Grace, I..."

"Yes, Babcock," Endymion said without a backwards glance at his long-suffering secretary. "That will be all."

"Thank you, Your Grace." From the clatter of his footsteps and the scrabbling noises at the door, Babcock had fled the room like the last fox in England upon hearing the baying of hounds.

Voil's laughter subsided only to start up once more when he looked from the letter to Endymion and back. Breathing in through his nose, Endymion flipped the slightly crimped missive over to peruse the duchess's latest reply.

To His Grace, Endymion Michael George de Waryn
Duke of Pendeen
Your Grace,
Thank you for your kind invitation. Again. It may be breeding season for dukes in London. As there has not been a duke of breeding age in Cornwall in my lifetime, I am unfamiliar with their breeding season here. And here is where I intend to remain.
Rhiannon Harvey de Waryn
Duchess of Pendeen

"What did you write to deserve such a response?" Voil sat up and drew a handkerchief from his pocket to wipe tears of laughter from his eyes.

Endymion stared at the piece of stationary crushed in his hand. He didn't remember closing his fist around it. Ignoring his friend, he returned to his desk and smoothed out the letter. On the shelf directly behind him, he plucked the box marked *This Month's Correspondence Received* from its place and tucked the still wrinkled page inside it before returning the box to the shelf. At the end of the month, Babcock would file it away in the box reserved for the duke's correspondence with the duchess.

The duke's correspondence.

With the duchess.

Until a month ago, he'd not written a single letter to his wife of seventeen years. He'd left that task to his uncle. In spite of the many reasons that had arisen for Endymion himself to correspond with his interests in Cornwall, perhaps he should have left this chore to his uncle. What had possessed Endymion to write to her now? He stared at the rows and rows of boxes as if they might hold the answer.

"If you cannot recall what you wrote, for God's sake, man, can you tell me why you wrote to her after all this time?"

He faced Voil, still seated on the sofa but more alert than he'd seen him in years. Alert and...pitying. Hell! This was not to be borne. Endymion lifted the book by which he conducted his life, strode to the sofa, and dropped the leather volume into his startled friend's lap. A singular honor. Few people beyond Babcock and Endymion's butler, Vaughn, had been allowed the privilege he now afforded the Marquess of Voil.

"You cannot tell me the old bastard ordered you when to..." Voil stopped leafing through the pages of the schedule book and slowly raised his head. "Please tell me you did not invite your duchess to London in order to— Good God, you did." He tossed the book onto the table before the sofa.

"Did what?" This conversation was about to take a road Endymion did not want to travel. Not even with his oldest friend. Too many roads in his mind led to dangerous places. Places he had put behind him. Places he had no memory of and no desire to visit to regain those memories.

"Hell and the devil, man, you're still living your life by your grandfather's rules. He's dead, Pendeen. You're alive. You can make your own rules."

"I know I'm alive." Endymion collapsed into one of the high-backed leather chairs before his desk.

"Do you? I've seen little evidence of it, especially since the old man stuck his spoon in the wall. I know bluestocking spinsters who've had more fun. They don't hang you for breaking the rules."

"You will forgive me if I decline to take advice about rules from a man with little to no acquaintance with them." Endymion resisted the urge to scrub his hands over his face.

Voil grinned. "On the contrary, I have an intimate acquaintance with them. I use the rules to live the most scandalous life possible without offending anyone. You use the rules as a place to hide."

"Ridiculous." He rolled his shoulders and slouched down into the chair. "What have I to hide from?"

"I don't know, but if that letter is an example of her response to your wooing talents, I suggest you hide from your duchess, for starters." Voil slid down on the sofa, mimicking Endymion's posture.

"You are not helping."

"At least, until the breeding season for dukes is over."

"Nor are you amusing in the least."

"Very well, Your Grace." Voil snatched the leather-bound book from the table and tossed it at Endymion. "What does His Late Grace's book say you should do next?"

CHAPTER 2

Pendeen, Cornwall
August, 1814

JOSIAH THOMAS TURNED HIS HEAD AND SPAT ONTO THE packed dirt of the farmyard. "Missed him, Your Grace. Damned shame, that."

The disadvantage to firing one of Manton's double-barrel percussion fowling pieces was the dust and debris it stirred up when one took a shot at a man who deserved it. The advantage was not having to take the time to reload before the second shot. Once one had a clear line to the target.

"I didn't miss, Josiah." Rhiannon Harvey de Waryn, Duchess of Pendeen, snugged the butt of the long gun into her shoulder and blinked her target into focus past the mixed cloud of gunpower and flying dirt. "I was giving him a chance to run."

A chorus of guffaws and jeers erupted from her mines manager and the grooms and footmen who'd accompanied her on the long ride from *Gorffwys Ddraig*, the seat of the Pendeen duchy, to the Wilson tenant farm at the far end of the estate. The corner of Rhiannon's mouth kicked up even as a sprinkling of sweat popped out on her upper lip. She steadied her grip on the Manton and inhaled slightly. Her palms remained dry and her hands steady. Thank God for small mercies. At a mere four inches over five feet tall, with a slender frame she despised for its lack of curves, wit and poise and her tenacious grip on calm were often all that kept her on her feet.

"She's a right'un, is our duchess."

"I'd do as she says, lad. Her Grace don't miss, 'specially when she's vexed."

"S-she's mad is what s-she is." Robert Wilson windmilled his skinny arms to dispel the last of the smoke encircling his florid face. "Captain Randolph is the steward here, Josiah Thomas, not you. T-take your *arse* back to the mines and t-take her with you. S-she has no right to shoot at me on my own p-property."

Neither lowering the gun nor altering her aim, Rhiannon took a step toward the spluttering excuse for a farmer. He backed up and tried to hide behind his wife. The care-worn woman with the black eye and split lip shifted the babe on her hip and pushed her husband away with her splinted arm.

"It isn't your property, is it, Robert? And it isn't Captain Randolph's." Rhiannon took another step and heard her men close ranks behind her. "It's mine. And I'll have no wife beaters here. You have fifteen minutes to clear out." She thumbed back the hammer of the unspent barrel. She tried not to see his wife's battered face, the wide-eyed stares of the brood of children—barefoot in ragged clothes—huddled behind their mother. The heat of unspoken fury swept up her body—most of it directed at the loud-mouthed drunkard gaping at her like a fish landed on a riverbank. Most of it.

"She's mine to beat."

"Not anymore." Rhiannon blew the hair from her eyes. "Fourteen minutes."

"Who will work this land? Who will look after my family if you banish me?"

"The same person who always has." She glanced at the gangly youth of some fifteen odd years who stared at his father with the placid contempt born of a lifetime of abuse. "Agreed, Young Bob?"

"Yes, Your Grace," the boy said softly as he stepped in front of his mother. He raised his chin a notch. "Agreed." Rhiannon fought the urge to smile. Young lads who had just become men did not brook tender emotions, no matter how richly deserved. She knew this from bitter experience. With a solemn nod, she turned her attention back to his infuriated sire.

"You have no right to take a man's wife. His children. Duchess or not. A man has rights." Fists clenched and half-raised, Wilson started forward. Rhiannon lowered her aim to the man's crotch as she heard the men at her back shout and scramble, prepared to intervene.

"I doubt anyone here sees the least thing in you that even hints at a man." Rhiannon met her target halfway, close enough to press the end of the Manton to his filthy, torn wool breeches. Her mind screamed *"Danger!"* but she refused to blink. Seventeen years as de facto mistress of this estate, seven years as the sole authority over the largest duchy in three counties, had taught her the power of a fearless demeanor. Even when circumstances had her shaking in her half boots. "One more step and I'll geld you and remove all doubt."

Even the chickens scratching in vain at the impregnable dirt ceased their futile search for food. This close to the sea, yet not a breeze stirred the summer heat. Rhiannon's cotton stockings stuck to her legs. The weight of her kerseymere skirts dragged at her waist. Her tightly braided hair, coiled on top and at the back of her head, threatened to slip its pins. Half a dozen lines of icy sweat meandered down her back. The men behind her shifted a bit. It had taken time and determination for her to train them to trust her to command a situation until she asked for their help. She took great pride in their scarcely reined patience, palpable, at this point.

"You'll get yours, bitch," Wilson growled, so only she might hear. The quake to his voice and the widening of his eyes belied his faith in those words.

"Perhaps I will, but as I'm the bitch with the gun, I won't be getting it from you." With a confidence ready to flee over the distant cliffs at any moment, Rhiannon lowered the Manton, showed him her back, and walked away. "Your lease is terminated, Robert Wilson," she tossed over her shoulder. "John, Jack, escort this vermin off the estate. If he steps onto any Pendeen-held property, he's to be shot on sight."

Two tall, broad footmen dressed in simple black and white livery strode past Rhiannon. She turned when she reached Josiah's side and watched as they hooked Wilson beneath the arms and dragged him kicking and cursing to the empty hay wagon at the edge of the farmyard. They had him trussed and thrown into the wagon bed in a thrice. With a brief bow to Rhiannon, John and Jack hopped onto the back next to their prisoner. A short whistle from the wizened gnome of a driver set the team of draft horses in the traces into motion.

"I don't like it, Your Grace." Josiah stared after the wagon, his hand combing the wiry curls of his silver-grey beard.

"Which part?" Rhiannon handed the Manton off to one of the grooms and stepped into the hands of another as he helped her mount Selene. None too soon, either. Her legs, weak and wavy as water, had threatened to give way from the moment she'd fired that first shot. From atop her mare, the earth solidified beneath her. "The part where I threatened to shoot him or the part where he called me a bitch?"

"He what?" Josiah snatched the Manton from the groom and started after the wagon.

"Oh, for pity's sake." Rhiannon urged her mare forward and

plucked the gun from her mines manager's hands. "He's not the first man to call me a bitch. I daresay, he won't be the last."

Her father's faithful steward and friend, Josiah Thomas, had known her from infancy. He'd watched over her the nearly thirty-one years of her life, especially since her father's death. He was protective of the girl she'd been. He was ferociously so of the duchess she'd become. Looking out for him settled her nerves and allowed her a moment to gather her wits. A moment she sorely needed.

"You're a lady," the young groom observed as he came to check the security of her boot in the stirrup. "The Duchess of Pendeen. He has no right to call you anything at all, 'cept Your Grace."

"Even this lad knows what's proper," Josiah grumbled as he alternated his gaze between the Manton in the crook of her arm and the wagon disappearing up the road.

"Yes, well," Rhiannon adjusted her skirts over the pommel of her sidesaddle and took up the reins the groom handed her. "I didn't threaten to shoot *the lad's* tarrywags off, did I?"

The young groom grinned. "No, Your Grace. And I thank you."

She handed him the Manton. "Reload it and bring it along. And don't let Mr. Thomas near it, lest he decide to reopen season on some portion of Robert Wilson's anatomy."

At Josiah's signal, another groom stepped in and began to inspect the girth and bridle on Rhiannon's horse. The lad checked and rechecked every strap and buckle. After several minutes of such nonsense, Rhiannon had had enough.

"That will do, Davy. In spite of Mr. Thomas's nanny tendencies, I am perfectly capable of sitting a horse."

"Not even you can sit a horse when the tack has been cut," Josiah declared as he waved Davy away and took over the inspection himself.

"It wasn't cut. It was an accident, a simple accident." Rhiannon told herself so every day. She had to.

"As you say, Your Grace." Josiah spat, jammed his hat on his head, and crossed the yard to mount his horse.

She urged her horse toward Mrs. Wilson and her children.

"Should have killed him." Young Bob stared at his mother's injuries. He twisted a threadbare cap in his hands. "I wish you had." His voice fell to a husky whisper and his eyes shone with unshed tears. "I wish I had."

"If I had, I'd have to make an appointment with the magistrate, a dull old stick of a man who would natter at me for hours. If you had, you'd have to make an appointment with the rope. Quicker and far less dull, but still a bother." She met his gaze and held it. "Your father isn't worth all that trouble. Don't you agree?"

He dragged his sleeve across his eyes. "Yes, Your Grace."

"Meg," she addressed the pale woman who gazed up the now empty road as if to make certain the source of her torment was truly gone. "You make a list of what you need in the way of repairs and supplies. I'll have them sent down from *Gorffwys Ddraig*." Rhiannon studied the half dozen children peering past their mother and elder brother. "And some food."

"We've no money to pay for it, Your Grace." Meg pushed the greying blonde hair away from her eyes. "Had no money for nigh on these six months."

Rhiannon patted Selene's neck to settle the mare's nervous dancing in place. "We'll settle it after the harvest." A wordless communication passed between them. The woman was no older than herself, though she looked at least ten years her senior. Dressed in over-mended clothes, wearing the marks of her husband's brutality, Meg Wilson still had her pride. The Duchess of Pendeen knew all too well, sometimes pride alone kept a woman going when life took everything else away. When men took everything else away.

"Come up to *Gorffwys Ddraig* tomorrow, lad." Josiah drew his horse to a halt next to the wiry child so rudely thrust into manhood. "We'll make a plan to right this farm and see you through the winter."

Young Bob tugged his forelock and nodded.

In a dusty clatter of hooves and jingling tack, Rhiannon and her men put the Wilson farm behind them. They'd reached the main road and ridden over halfway across Pendeen's vast holdings before anyone spoke again.

"Did those lamps from Mr. Davy's arrive?" Rhiannon refused to dwell on the events of the past hour. It didn't do to chew the same meat twice. She'd had a problem. She'd dispatched it to her satisfaction. Time to move on to the next. And there was always a next. In fact, there was one very big *next*. She'd had no luck in sweeping it from her mind, either.

"They did." Josiah urged his gelding to keep pace with Selene. The towering gorse hedges on either side of the road blocked the sudden gusts that pushed in from the sea. The sky portended a coming storm, still far enough off for them to make it to *Gorffwys Ddraig* so long as they didn't dawdle. "The miners don't fancy them."

"I don't fancy digging men out after another explosion. I've studied his design. It's sound. He sent the lamps to be tested and that's what we're going to do." The walls of gorse subsided into walls of stone, walls low enough to reveal the hills on either side of the road dotted with grazing sheep. Spring lambs, nearly half-grown now, leapt and butted each other amongst the rocks and grass of the pastures. Rhiannon smiled at their play.

"Sent them at no charge?"

"Of course."

Josiah snorted. "You are your father's daughter."

Rhiannon laughed. She and her father had their troubles when he was alive, but she'd truly mourned his death. At least, he had stayed. Even when she'd wished him gone, he'd stayed.

The passage of time made it easier to remember his good qualities, and as for the bad... Well, dead loved ones didn't make mistakes. Neither did absent ones. When they stayed absent. Now was not the time to revisit that particular mistake.

"He'll be trouble, Your Grace."

Rhiannon started. "Who, Josiah?"

"Wilson. He'll not let his banishment stand. He'll be back."

"Perhaps." Rhiannon suppressed a sigh of relief. She coaxed her mare into a trot as they turned into the open gates at the head of the drive to Pendeen's sprawling ancestral pile. The rampant Pendeen dragons, poised in carved defiance on either side of the main gates, appeared nearly alive in the dappled sunlight. The trees in full leaf on either side blocked the light fading in the wake of the coming rain. It made for a long, cool ride—one fraught with memory, of dreams and nightmares. Yet, even with the things she'd rather forget, she loved this place, her home. The land, the village, the tenant farms, the mines and fields and pastures. The people. And the magnificent house coming into view as they topped the hill. She loved it all because it was hers. It was what she had made it and no man could take that from her. Not even the one man she'd hoped would at least try. *If wishes were horses...*

"No perhaps to it, Your Grace. Vermin like him tends to creep back in when you least expect it." Josiah reined in his horse beside hers. The horses behind them stopped, as well.

She always paused here, at the crest of the drive, to drink in the sight of the ornate finial-topped turrets and ranks of lancet windows set into the bowed arches across the façade of *Gorffwys Ddraig*, Dragon's Rest, the home of the Dukes of Pendeen for over six hundred years. Manicured lawns rolled down to meet lush gardens set before the house in a studied chaos that gave the appearance of barely trained wilderness. A wall of yew trees, planted by the de Waryn family's Norman ancestors, stood at the edge of a ha-ha, blocking *Gorffwys Ddraig* from view until the last minute. The house itself, crafted of stone in hues of dun yellow and marbled white, sprawled across the shallow valley in an eerie array of castellated walls, covered walkways, and expansive parapets.

As a child, Rhiannon was frightened by the monstrous combination of medieval castle and gothic cathedral that was *Gorffwys Ddraig*. The one time she'd sought to explore it alone she'd become hopelessly lost. That night had not ended well. For anyone. At fourteen still very much a child, she'd become the mistress of the de Waryn family seat, and for the last seventeen years she'd had nothing but time to learn the house's many secrets. She'd claimed every part of it, swept away the darkness and replaced it with light. *Nos defendere nostra* was the de Waryn family motto. *We defend our own.* She lived her life by it, even if no other de Waryn chose to do so.

"We've never had trouble ridding ourselves of vermin before, Josiah. I don't intend to start now." Rhiannon pressed her heel to Selene's side and shifted her weight back in the sidesaddle as they started down the drive. They cleared the shade of the trees and turned toward the cobblestoned carriageway that led to the covered front portico.

"Even if it comes in a regiment of carriages?"

"What are you..." Rhiannon had been so caught up in the web of remembrance woven into the very walls of *Gorffwys Ddraig*, she had not seen the four crested carriages and baggage wagon lined up before the front doors of the house. Until it was too late.

He'd done it.

He'd actually done the one thing he'd vowed never in his life to do.

Damn him.

"Give me the gun, Dickie." She thrust her hand back toward the groom to whom she'd handed over the Manton.

He'd no sooner placed it in her hand than Josiah made a

grab for it. "Shooting Wilson is one thing, Your Grace. Shooting a peer of the realm is something else entirely."

"Depends on the peer." She tugged the fowling piece free and whistled Selene into a canter down the carriageway. Rhiannon ignored the startled shouts and clattering hooves that set Josiah and the others in pursuit. Footmen in two different sets of livery scattered out of the portico to avoid being run down. Fortunately, Tall William, one of her footmen, came down the steps in time to catch her as she slid from her sidesaddle. "Where is he?"

"Your Grace?" The footman frowned in confusion as he handed Selene off to a waiting stable boy. Swarming around them, under the direction of a sparrow of a man dressed in immaculate black, servants in blue and gold livery carted trunks and boxes from the carriages and wagon into the house. Josiah and the rest of her men rode under the portico, adding to the noise and chaos.

"Think before you go in there, Your Grace," Josiah warned as he swung off his gelding and pushed through the crowd of horses and servants.

Rhiannon snorted and marched through the open double doors. She'd done nothing but think since the night he'd fled Cornwall like a thief in the night. Their wedding night.

"I beg your pardon, Your Grace." Vaughn, who had been the butler at Pendeen long before the old duke's death, hurried across the entrance hall. "I didn't know what to do with…" His voice dropped even as he jerked his head in the direction of the first-floor landing, "*Him*."

"Good afternoon, Your Grace," said the very last man she ever expected to return to Cornwall. He deigned to offer her a brief inclination of his head.

With her hand on her hip and the Manton in the crook of her other arm, Rhiannon tilted her head up toward the sound of that voice. *That* voice. The tall man in the black Hessians, buff-colored buckskin breeches, and dark blue hunting jacket was unknown to her—save for the green eyes, the cleft in his chin, the dark mahogany hair still prone to curl at his nape, and that deep, starless night of a damned voice. She cleared her features of all expression and narrowed her eyes, all in aid of quieting the eruption of emotion roiling through her.

"What are you doing here, Dymi?" She bit back a curse at the husky catch in her throat.

A touch of condescending amusement crossed the sharp edges of his face. He rested his hand on the marble balustrade. "You wouldn't come to London for duke season, so I've brought duke season to you." His lips curled in a stoic half-smile. "You're welcome."

CHAPTER 3

With the abrupt force of cold water over a drunkard's head, silence, blessed silence, descended over the roiling cacophony of the entrance hall. Endymion repressed the sigh of relief his body fought so violently to release. A Duke of Pendeen did not experience relief, and he certainly never displayed relief in public.

He let the quiet fill him, a skill he'd learned under his grandfather's tutelage. In his determination to enter the house as if he'd never been away, he'd not noticed the massive medieval entrance hall. Until now. It had been changed. Or, at least, he believed it had. He had a vague idea of animal heads—dead eyes of stags, boar, wolves—staring at him from walls grey with smoke and ash above dingy oak paneling. The hunting trophies were gone. The walls had been whitewashed, the woodwork polished to a rich glow.

"Get out, whore, and take your bastards with you. There will never be a place for your sort here."

The low, insistent clang of memories just out of reach had plagued him from the moment he'd crossed the river into Cornwall. Like the buzzing of bees angered by his intrusion where he had no business, the faint insistent hum of events he could not recall had crawled along his skin and filled his head nigh on to madness. His arrival at the Pendeen family seat had only made the howling specter of his amorphous nightmares worse.

He dug his thumbnail into his palm. The past had no place in the present. He'd made no attempt to retrieve those months before he'd been dragged away from this place and its haunting, faceless fears. Still, that voice, a voice he knew but didn't know, reached out of the mist, ever seeking to claim him. Until he fixed his gaze on her, the single person in the stupefied multitude standing below him who refused to look away.

His own servants were trained to work quietly and efficiently so as not to intrude on Endymion's ordered life. The servants in Cornwall had no such compunction. Apparently, the arrival of a duke gave cause for a great deal of shouting, a great deal of running about, and the sort of chaos he'd only endured at a ball when a young lady fainted dead away at Endymion's request for a dance. A request he'd only made because the hostess, an elderly countess with a particularly shrill voice, had insisted. The ensuing riot had sped his departure from the ball, considerably shortening his scheduled one-hour attendance. He had no such departure planned here.

Voil's damned pungent cologne announced his approach long before his sudden arrival on the first-floor landing, thereby spoiling Voil's attempt to startle Endymion. "Two questions, Your Grace."

"I will not brook complaints now, Voil. You would come, invited or not." In spite of the momentary cessation of noise, Endymion flexed his hands against the steady thrum of clamoring ghosts.

"I suspect these next weeks shall be far more entertaining than anything happening in London," Voil said softly, even as he nudged Endymion's back with his elbow. "What the devil did you say?"

"Say?" Endymion said absently. He kept his gaze on the one person who dared look him in the eye in defiance and barely leashed fury. The person on whom he'd focused to calm the pounding in his head. And it worked. His hands relaxed. His shoulders, strung like a bow, settled beneath his coat.

"What did you say to them?"

"I don't recall." He did. She'd asked him a question. His response had infuriated her. And dammit, he saw at once the one thing he'd never given a moment's thought to during the long journey from London. The gangly, barely fourteen-year-old girl he'd been forced to marry had grown into a duchess. His vision of the girl was blurry, at best. Rhiannon Harvey de Waryn, however, stood as the clearest image in an entire county of faded, swirling people and places.

"You don't recall?" Voil asked in mock horror. "I take it the lady at whom you are staring like a lovesick schoolboy is your long-lost wife?"

"She was never lost," Endymion murmured as he started down the stairs. As if by prior design, Babcock snapped his fingers at the footmen they'd brought from London, who immediately returned to the task of unloading the luggage and carrying it to the duke's suite on the second floor. The Cornwall staff jumped into motion as well, with far more chatter and far less organization.

"Your pardon. Merely misplaced for seventeen years," Voil replied. "You never mentioned she was beautiful. And armed."

"Stay here," Endymion ordered as they reached the bottom of the stairs.

"She has a gun," Voil observed. "*Bon chance, mon frere.*"

Endymion crossed the polished marble floor. His Hessians beat a clipped tattoo until he stood before the woman he'd recognized the instant she'd entered the hall. Voil had teased him mercilessly that he would not. Endymion had secretly agreed, for reasons that had nothing to do with the time he'd absented himself from Cornwall. The time before his grandfather had spirited him away to London to hide behind a thick curtain of pain and a deliberate desire to leave the past where it belonged.

Some things—some people—defied pain and deliberation.

She narrowed her dark brown eyes, blew a strand of hair from her face, and tapped her foot twice. Endymion fought a smile. Her hair, so rich a brunette as to appear bronzed gold in certain lights, had ever been unruly, but never so silky as it shone now. She was still short and petite of frame, although with new curves, poured into a serviceable kerseymere walking dress, that provoked some surprising physical reactions in him. The gold flecks in those changeable dark eyes flashed fire. He'd been standing there staring and it provoked the devil out of her. That much was clear. Very little else was, save that concentrating on his previously ignored duchess held the encroaching walls of the house at bay.

"Did you come all this way merely to upset my household and stare at me like some overdressed looby?"

"We both know why I am here, do we not?" he replied.

"Because, in spite of receiving the finest education that the best tutors and the dons at Oxford had to offer, you have yet to learn the meaning of the word *No*?"

Several snickers whispered around the cavernous entrance hall. Endymion cut his gaze sharply to survey the servants, her servants, pretending to be about their work. He received solemn faces, curtsies, and a few pulled forelocks in return.

"Perhaps a private conversation is in order," he suggested.

"What could we possibly have to say to one another, *Your Grace?*" She cocked her head, the mutinous set of her jaw so familiar as to tilt Endymion's hard-won dignity. The light of the setting sun reached through the tall windows behind them and glanced off the barrel of the gun slung across her left arm. An armed duchess did not do a great deal for his dignity either. Especially this duchess.

"We have much to discuss once we dispense with this." Endymion reached for the Manton. A far away roar echoed in his ears. He shuddered. Ice crept from his fingertips up his arm until he simply froze, mid-reach. Waves of sound, a noise he often heard in his dreams, broke over him. His lungs refused to draw breath. *Oh, God. Not now.*

"Tall William?" Rhiannon said, her voice miraculously breaking the spell.

"Yes, Your Grace?" A lanky, raw-boned footman in stark black-and-white livery hurried to her side.

"Take this and put it away." She handed off the weapon without a glance in the footman's direction. Instead, she fixed on Endymion, her eyes liquid and soft. She sighed, a sad sound, and suddenly Endymion regained the ability to breathe.

"Are you sure, Your Grace?" the footman asked as he conducted a disdainful perusal of Endymion's person.

She smiled. "For now. Come along, Your Grace." With a wave of her hand, she started down a long, paneled corridor that passed under the staircase to the right.

Endymion watched the cheeky footman walk away. Something about a man in black livery, the precise tap of his footsteps across the marble entrance hall, pushed past the walls of indifference he rushed to bolster. For a blink of a moment, a weight of sorrow and fear struck him a glancing blow. Out of here. He needed out of here.

Halfway down the corridor, his duchess peered over her shoulder at him. "You aren't afraid to be alone with me, are you, Your Grace?" In any of the women who'd wasted their time pursuing Endymion nearly from the moment he'd arrived in London as an awkward, sickly youth, her expression might be considered flirtatious. He'd been married to her for seventeen years, knew her not at all, and yet he'd wager his life she did not flirt. Ever.

"Terrified," he assured her as he followed her down the corridor. "I shall, however, endeavor to be brave. Returning to my home after such a long absence might prove problematic if I cry craven on the first day."

She snorted. "Invading *my* home after such a long absence may prove more than problematic. This way."

RHIANNON STEADIED HER STEPS. SHE REFUSED TO HURRY simply because his long legs allowed him to cover the distance between them in a few strides. She'd not look back again either. No need really, as his tall, muscled body loomed behind her near enough to touch. She breathed in his clean, masculine scent and immediately chastised herself for her folly.

She'd been infatuated with *the handsome lad*, as everyone had called him, a harmless girlhood fancy. The man who'd finally returned to Cornwall was anything but harmless. His was the austere, striking sort of male beauty destined to break hearts. His heart had been broken long ago and it was not her place to repair it. Indeed, she'd almost decided he no longer had one to break. Until today.

His reaction to the gun had done it, dash it all. For a moment, Endymion stood before her—fifteen years old, in the throes of a confused anguish and fear he didn't understand. Or, perhaps it was all for show, to gain her sympathy. He'd been his grandfather, the duke's, creature for ten years and then the grandfather's brother, Lord Richard de Waryn, had taken over the task of ensuring her husband acted the perfect, all-powerful peer. Rhiannon did not trust her husband's uncle. She dared not trust her husband. Not until she learned who Endymion the man had become and why he'd finally returned to Cornwall.

"What did you do with the heads?" Endymion breached the silence to ask as they reached her study.

Rhiannon, her hand on the eight-panel oak door, looked over her shoulder at him. "The heads?" Seventeen years away, and he asked her about...heads?

"The duke's trophies in the front hall. They're gone." His face was unreadable, but his voice gave him away. The depth and richness that time had added did not deceive her. He was puzzled, and he did not like it.

"Very observant of you, Your Grace." Rhiannon stepped into her study and marched to the ornate, broad oak desk across from the massive fireplace. She perched on the edge of the overstuffed leather chair behind the desk and layered her arms along the intricately carved dragons that served as its arms. Spine erect, she adopted her *duchess* posture.

"You are the Duchess of Pendeen, my girl. Don't you forget it and never, ever let them forget it. You act like a duchess, they'll treat you like one."

Her father's words had burnt into her memory the morning after her wedding—the morning she awoke to find her new husband, his grandfather, his uncle, and every member of the duke's London household gone.

Her husband's return was no time to allow her father's lessons to go to waste. Her duchess demeanor appeared to be working, as Endymion stood in the doorway and perused the study as if he surveyed a foreign country. Good. A man off-balance was a man who might reveal his secrets.

"This room is changed, as well," he observed, still rooted in the doorway.

"So much so you cannot find your way inside?"

He frowned, clasped his hands behind his back, and strolled casually across the Persian carpets that covered the dark wood floor. Halfway through a circuit of the room, he stopped to study the painting over the fireplace at the far end of the study. "Turner?" he inquired.

"A gift from my father. It is *Gorffwys Ddraig* from the ridge above the terrace gardens." What was he about? He had not come here to indulge in idle chatter and send uncomfortable tremors up and down her body.

"*Gorffwys*..." He mangled the old Cornish word. She nearly laughed at him, but it struck her. He truly did not remember.

"*Gorffwys Ddraig*," she pronounced with care. "The name of this house in the old language." He'd done it again. Made her pity him. Enough. "Sit down, Your Grace, and state the purpose for this visit. I have correspondence to answer and some accounts to look over before dinner." Rhiannon had cowed many a man with her brusque demeanor and iron-laced tone. Endymion had never been the sort to be cowed. He'd paid the price for his defiance in the worst manner imaginable. She could not allow her memories of the boy she'd grown up with to shake her now. No matter the ridiculous hopes she visited from time to time.

"I hear and obey." He inclined his head. A flitter of amusement crossed his face. He traversed the room with quieter steps and far more elegant grace than a man his size allowed. Once he'd subsided into one of the chairs before her desk, he leaned back and stretched his legs out before him, his fingers laced across the black and gold silk brocade of his waistcoat. Unfortunately, the taut muscles in his face, his neck, and his hands gave him away. An image of the easy, assured boy he'd been came unbidden to her mind.

"You haven't obeyed anyone since you were nine." Rhiannon crossed her arms and took a deep breath. "Why are you here?"

"You have grown quite lovely, Duchess. More lovely than I remember."

"I was fourteen when last you saw me. How fortunate for you I have not grown uglier. You are still too damned tall, but, at least, the food in London agrees with you. In addition to not having learned the meaning of the word *no*, you have also failed to learn how to answer a question."

He quirked an eyebrow. What a strange pass they had come to after all these years apart. She'd envisioned his homecoming many ways, when her firm vow not to think on him gave way. Her visions had never been this cold, civil exchange.

He sat up and adjusted his waistcoat. "It is time, madam. We have both reached an age where we are mature enough to do our duty to Pendeen."

"Our duty to Pendeen?" Rhiannon seethed, the heat of her anger pulsing in her veins. "I have been doing my duty to Pendeen these seventeen years, *Your Grace*. Whilst you have larked about London, made a name for yourself in Parliament, and danced at far more balls than I can credit for a man who once declared dancing *a monumental bloody waste of time*."

The hard line of his mouth relaxed, but he caught himself before he actually smiled. Rhiannon kicked her foot beneath her desk. She'd said too much. Again. She, who'd learned the hard way to measure every word, had become a magpie.

"I cannot help but be flattered—"

"Don't," she snapped. "This is Cornwall, not darkest Africa. We do receive the London papers."

"I see," he said quietly, eyebrows raised.

"Do you? Part of my duties as the Duchess of Pendeen is to know what the Duke of Pendeen has been up to *before* the neighbors do. Unfortunately, the newspapers have been my sole source of information as you have never troubled yourself to write, and your grandfather's brother only writes with complaints and requests for the estate's receipts." She swallowed hard against the lump around her heart rising into her throat.

"I charged Lord de Waryn with overseeing matters here at

Pendeen." Endymion's face remained blank. They might have been discussing the weather.

"I am not a *matter*, Dymi. I am your wife, in name, at least. One wonders why you have bothered to come to Cornwall, at all. Why not simply send Uncle Richard to dispatch your duty to Pendeen?"

Endymion rose and clasped his hands behind his back. "Don't be vulgar."

"Vulgar?" Rhiannon tugged open one of her desk drawers and fished out a letter. She tossed it across the desk. "Vulgar is asking your wife to come to London to be serviced by you like a broodmare until she is with child, at which point, she can toddle off home. And can she please do so before Parliament sits again in November."

He glanced at the letter. A slight flush splashed across his sharp cheekbones for a moment. He cleared his throat. "I have been informed my letter was...not the most romantic of missives."

Rhiannon snorted. "I have read ore quality reports more romantic." She pushed herself out of her chair and walked around the desk. Once she stood toe to toe with him, she tilted her head back to meet his gaze. "Why are you really here?"

He reached out, slowly, and ran a loose lock of her hair between his finger and thumb. "Your curls are not as wild as they once were."

"It has taken all her considerable powers, but my lady's maid, Beatrice, has tamed them." The scar across his thumb had faded.

"Pity," he said softly as he released her hair and quickly clasped his hands behind his back once more. "Rhee...Duchess, I—"

For a moment, he was almost the Dymi with whom she'd run the moors.

"My name is not Duchess," she snapped, without knowing why. "I am not a spaniel dog."

"You are the Duchess of Pendeen," he declared, as if she was not aware of it every waking moment of every day.

"Your letter is not the only unromantic thing about you, Your Grace," she said and stepped back. She bumped into the front of the desk, and this time he did smile.

"Perhaps you could show me how to be romantic." He raised his hand toward her face.

Rhiannon rolled her eyes and batted his hand away. "The only thing I wish to show you is the way back to London."

"Is there a reason you insist on my immediate departure? Perhaps I should"—he reached around her and plucked the open ledger book from her desk—"check the accounts."

She snatched the book from his hand. "I am working on these. You may check them once they are complete." The rough brush of his fingertips caused her stomach to flip.

A sharp rap sounded at the door.

"That will be my mines manager. If you will excuse me, he and I have business to discuss." Rhiannon dropped the ledger on the desk behind her and tried to walk away.

Endymion thrust his hand out to stop her. His hand. Which landed on her breast. Rhiannon looked into his green eyes. Shock. Surprise. Chagrin. And something she recognized, but dared not name, flashed across those jade depths.

"In case you are wondering," she started, "that"—she waved at his hand—"is even less romantic than your letter."

He snatched back the offending appendage. "We have to come to some sort of agreement...Rhiannon. For the good of the title, and all of the privileges afforded us, there is a price to pay."

A price to pay? If he said one more word, she would not be responsible for her actions.

Rap! Rap! Rap!

She took Endymion's arm and, with a good deal of tugging and nudging, escorted him out the door. Josiah, with a nod and a *Your Grace* for each of them, took that opportunity to duck into the study and make his way to the window across the room. Rhiannon turned her attention back to her utterly astonished husband.

"Dinner is at seven," she informed him. "We keep country hours. And unless you packed your French chef in all the baggage you dragged from London for a simple visit, it will be good Cornish fare. We have no taste for fancy food here."

"French chef? How do you know I have a—"

Rhiannon shut the door and shot the bolt home to lock it.

"Madam, open this door. Open this door at once." Something very like a kick from a Hessian boot struck the thick wood. Twice. "You are no spaniel, Duchess, you are a bulldog." A series of raised mutterings accompanied his footsteps down the corridor. She distinctly heard the words *stubborn woman* and smiled.

"I wouldn't smile, were I you, Your Grace. He's well within his rights to knock the door down," Josiah observed, his face not quite scowling, but close. "You will have to settle all of this eventually."

Rhiannon collapsed into her desk chair and pushed absently at some papers. "He won't kick the door down. He suffers from a fatal disease that precludes such brutish behavior."

"What disease would that be?"

"More than half his life with his grandfather and his uncle have infected him with a tragic case of being a gentleman."

"And if the Cornish air cures him of this disease?"

"I may be forced to declare open season on the ducal tarrywags."

Josiah roared with laughter. When he was done, however, he wiped his face with his voluminous handkerchief and lowered himself into the chair her husband had unwillingly vacated. "Will you tell him about the tack...and the ruins?"

"Tell him what? I have no wish to remind His Grace of the clumsy girl he married."

"A child falling from trees and into ponds is a far cry from a duchess being pushed from—"

"I was not pushed. I fell. Nothing more." Rhiannon had far bigger problems to consider than a few random accidents.

"You have to show him the account books, Your Grace." Josiah took the hint and changed the subject to the matter at hand.

"I know. The only question is, which set of books do I show him?"

CHAPTER 4

"Traitors," his duchess muttered as Endymion escorted her past the footmen lined up along the dining room wall.

"Is something amiss, Your Grace?" he asked as he seated her in the chair to the left of his at the head of the table.

"Not at all." Her forced smile and gracious demeanor did not fool him for a moment. Endymion's arrival had thrown his wife's entire life into turmoil. From the way she flounced into the carved cherrywood chair and glowered at the perfectly appointed table, the Duchess of Pendeen was in high dudgeon. And it suited her. Rather, it suited *Rhiannon*, the girl he'd known long ago. He wasn't quite certain who his duchess was. *Rhiannon*. Why was he so reluctant to use her name?

Attired in a simple green silk gown that bared her shoulders and fell in a straight line to the floor, she looked every inch the duchess. Her hair, done in a series of tightly wound braids atop her head added a few inches to her height. For some reason, that made Endymion smile.

"You set a lovely table, Your Grace." Voil, seated across from her on Endymion's right, waved his hand to indicate the rich linen-covered, formally set expanse that stretched down most of the room.

"Thank you, Lord Voil," she replied as she peered around the large silver epergne, two dragons rampant against a medieval tower, in an attempt to see the marquess. "But it is my servants who set the table. They appear to have emptied the silver closet and the entire butler's pantry to do so."

Endymion draped his serviette across his lap and caught the conspiratorial grin Voil shot him. No doubt, the lady had instructed the servants not to change a thing simply because His Grace was in residence. Those selfsame servants had taken it upon themselves to bedeck the table with the finest Sevres, the daintiest crystal, and the de Waryn family silver. Endymion recognized the silver, which matched the set with which he dined at the London townhouse.

"This oxtail soup is incomparable, Your Grace," Voil offered, leaning from one side of the epergne to the other. "Better than any I have had in London."

"I will be certain to pass your compliments on to Cook," Rhiannon replied. She tilted her head from side to side around the epergne in complete opposition to Voil's, as if they played an adult version of some child's game.

Endymion attended his soup. Voil was correct. It was delicious, as was the mackerel in gooseberry sauce, which accompanied it. The food kindled embers of memory. It tasted familiar, but distantly so. Why could he not shake this sensation of being smothered and then allowed to breathe, only to smother once more?

"Tall William," Rhiannon snapped, drawing Endymion from his reverie. "Please remove this eyesore from the table."

"Eyesore, Your Grace?" The footman she'd handed the gun to earlier, now dressed in spotless black and white livery, stepped away from the wall and scanned the table.

"This...thing." She waved at the epergne. "I refuse to bob about like a duck in search of breadcrumbs at my own dinner table."

"Yes, Your Grace." Tall William lifted the offending silver piece clear of the table and retreated behind the hidden door set into the wall at the far end of the dining room.

"It is called an *epergne*, and I doubt my grandfather would consider such an expensive piece an eyesore," Endymion said. Voil kicked him under the table.

"If your grandfather deigns to return from the grave to join us before dessert, I will have the *epergne* returned to the table," Rhiannon replied, her French flawless.

Voil choked on his soup. He waved off the footman who stepped forward to assist him. And still managed to rasp out "A hit!" between coughs.

Endymion, however, was not amused. His wife finished her soup and started on the mackerel. Eventually she sensed his eyes on her. She carefully placed her silverware across her plate and dabbed the serviette to the corners of her mouth. Her sensuous rose-colored mouth. Not that he noticed.

"That ducal glare might intimidate a pale London miss, Your Grace," Rhiannon said softly, "but I have stared down angry miners, wife-beating farmers, and any number of high-in-the-instep peers, your *arse* of a great uncle included. I am not afraid of you...Dymi."

Endymion leaned across the table and covered her hand with his. "I am pleased to hear it, Duchess. Fear is never a good basis for a marriage."

"Neither is two hundred and fifty miles and nearly two decades apart," she replied as she drew her hand from beneath his and lifted it to signal the removal for the next course.

Voil cleared his throat and kicked Endymion again for good measure. Why the devil had he allowed the man to accompany him? This entire venture was difficult enough without his friend's interference.

"I take it, you are not accustomed to dining in this"—Voil craned his neck to take in the entire room—"mausoleum."

Rhiannon laughed. "You have caught me out, Lord Voil. I usually take my meals in my study or in the family dining room."

Endymion conducted a surreptitious survey of the room, a room of which he had no recollection. The furnishings, cherry-wood dining chairs with deep blue and gold brocade upholstery, matched the expansive cherrywood dining table. Indeed, all the sideboards and commodes along the walls were also cherrywood and looked to be of Chippendale's design. The walls shone with gold embossed silk wallcovering, the floors with blue and gold Aubusson. A room as elegant and impersonal as any room in any house in Mayfair. His uncle had constantly disparaged the country home *"your country duchess"* kept as nothing short of a common wreck of a place. What other untruths had he told?

"I am not family," Voil prattled on, "but I much prefer dining in more intimate surroundings."

The footmen silently placed plates of roast beef with gravy, potatoes, carrots, and fluffy Yorkshire puddings before them. Endymion gave Voil a warning glance and tucked into the hot, aromatic course before him.

Family.

This house had never held a family. None that he remembered, at least. As he ate, Endymion glanced at the woman to whom he'd been married since she was a girl of fourteen. The woman he'd known since they were both in leading strings. A stranger. If she was uncomfortable sitting at this grand table under the watchful eye of a portrait of one of his female ancestors, he was even more so. His erect posture and impeccable table manners were all a show. He was ill at ease in his own skin, let alone in the hallowed halls of *Gorffwys Ddraig*, as she called it. And he would never let her know it, for fear she might use the knowledge against him.

Rhiannon did not fear him, but he found himself more than a little afraid of her. From the moment he laid eyes on her as she stormed into the foyer with a Manton fowling piece on her arm, two things slammed into him like a punch to the head when sparring with Gentleman Jackson himself. The first, his wife was far more alluring and complicated than he'd ever imagined. And second, being near her stirred a past to life he had no desire to revisit.

"I trust your journey here was a good one, Your Grace," his duchess inquired with an innocent smile he didn't trust.

"Tolerable," Endymion replied and returned attention to his plate. Voil groaned and kicked at him, but his aim failed. Endymion turned on the marquess and gave him the "*What?*" expression he'd employed when they attended Oxford and Voil discovered they were in trouble before he did.

"His journey may have been tolerable, but mine was not," Voil declared.

"Oh dear," she replied. "Why ever not?"

The lady was enjoying this entirely too much. Endymion had never mastered the art of idle chatter. Voil was an artist at it.

"Oh, your husband's coach is the very model of comfort," Voil said, warming to his story, "but he refuses to travel once the sun sets. He is most particular as to which inns he patronizes. And he refuses to allow a man food and drink in the confines of his conveyance."

By the time Voil finished his tale of woe, she was laughing softly, with her fingers pressed to her lips. Her shoulders, flattered by the cut of her green silk gown, shook beneath the light of the candelabra. "Surely not, Lord Voil."

"God's truth, Your Grace. The duke is a most disagreeable travel companion," Voil, the traitorous wretch, assured her.

"Defend yourself, Your Grace." Rhiannon signaled for the next course.

"I cannot, Madam," Endymion replied. "He is telling the truth. For once. At least, his version of it."

"And your version?" She touched her fingers to his hand, briefly. Not briefly enough, for her touch shot through him and lodged somewhere behind his ribs.

"Voil has never traveled farther west than Hampshire. He has no idea the dangers one might encounter on the less traveled roads at night. And I am too fond of my horses to allow them to break a leg for the sake of expedience." Endymion leaned back to allow the footmen to clear the course and set a spinach tart before him.

"What dangers? Did you imagine we'd be set upon by highwaymen?" Voil asked, waving a forkful of tart in the air. "There haven't been highwaymen in England for a dog's age."

A wave of heat, followed by a chilling cold, washed over Endymion. His head pulsed as if wrapped in wool. He carefully placed his silverware alongside his plate. His left hand slid to the top of his thigh where he pinched himself. Another technique his grandfather had taught him. A dainty hand curled around his beneath the table. He turned his head enough to see her face. Her smile, all amusement and cordiality, was for Voil. Her eyes, however, soft and deep and shining with the sort of understanding only a kindred spirit might know, were for Endymion alone.

"There are men far more evil than highwaymen wandering the roads, Lord Voil," she said. "Cornwall is not London."

"You as well, Your Grace?" Voil said in mock horror. "Of course, you and Pendeen grew up together, didn't you? With tales of ghosts and beasts on the moors."

"Really, my lord," Rhiannon said as she gave Endymion's hand a last squeeze. "We had no time for such nonsense when we were children. We were far too busy climbing trees and stealing Cook's mince pies."

"As I recall, you were busy falling out of trees, and I was busy catching you before you dashed your brains out on the ground," Endymion said dryly.

"How ungentlemanly of you to remember,' Rhiannon chided him. "And allowing me to land on top of you does not constitute catching me."

"His Grace, the Duke of Pendeen, stealing pies?" Voil asked with a silly grin.

Endymion rolled his eyes at the marquess. "I most certainly did not. I merely ate the pies Her Grace stole."

Voil roared with laughter.

Endymion caught the serviette she tossed at him.

"You, Your Grace," she declared indignantly, "should be ashamed of yourself. I was only able to steal the pies because you distracted Cook for me to do so."

"You both fared better than I," Voil groused. "I tried to have a meat pasty delivered to the coach when we stopped in St. Agnes. This one," he jerked a thumb at Endymion, "caught the maid I paid to sneak it to me, paid her, and told her to eat the pasty with his compliments."

"I trust this evening's dinner has made up for it," Endymion said as the footmen cleared the spinach tart and served orange pudding and trifle for dessert.

"Indeed, it has," Voil replied. "Superb repast. It almost makes up for my missing the chance to visit one of the most haunted taverns in England. 'Tis said they serve a fine ale there, and a tasty beef pasty too. Pendeen here refused to even entertain the notion of stopping."

Endymion took care to guide the spoonful of orange

pudding to his mouth. He chewed it thoroughly and allowed it to slide down his throat. No fire had been lit in the hearth beneath the carved marble mantelpiece. Cold crept over his evening shoes and up his legs, inches at a time, like the thick black water of the bogs between the village of Zennor and Pendeen. He continued to spoon the pudding into his mouth. His eyes wide open, he saw nothing.

Rhiannon's voice cut through the pounding roar in Endymion's ears. "There are no haunted taverns in Cornwall, Lord Voil. You've heard only gossip and children's tales to entertain visitors."

"Certainly, you have heard of it, Your Grace," Voil insisted. "It is not far from here, although your husband had his coachman take the long way around and missed it altogether. It is said the ghost of a beautiful tavern wench can be seen on moonlit nights. The tavern is The Mermaid's—"

"You are misinformed, my lord. There is no such tavern and no such ghost," Rhiannon snapped. She pushed her dish away so suddenly drops of trifle dropped onto the pristine linen tablecloth.

Endymion stared at those drops. He did not look at her, Rhiannon, his duchess. His lungs slowed. His heart raced. He didn't know why, not completely. But she did. He heard it in her voice—concern and pain on his behalf. He held his spoon until his knuckles blanched and continued to eat his pudding. And wished his best and only friend to the devil. Wished his grandfather to the devil for forcing him to return to Cornwall, even from beyond the grave.

The clink of his spoon at the bottom of the crystal dessert dish shook something loose in him. By rote, Endymion set his dish back. He wiped his mouth with the expensive linen serviette and placed it on the table next to the dish. The cherrywood chair slid silently across the Aubusson as he pushed it away from the table. He stood and finally turned to face Rhiannon. The look on her face cut him like a blade. The roar of a musket blast filled his mind.

"Pendeen?" Voil's voice was uncharacteristically serious.

"Dinner was most enjoyable, Duchess. Thank you." Endymion reached for his wife's hand, bowed over it, and in as dignified a manner as his shaky legs allowed, fled the room.

CHAPTER 5

Dressed in her oldest linen nightgown, with her hair brushed out and secured in one long braid down her back, Rhiannon tucked her feet beneath herself and breathed in the sweet summer air laced with the scents of lavender and roses. After the events of this day, she desperately needed the sanctuary of her favorite place and some time to contemplate...everything.

Rhiannon had many favorite places within the walls of *Gorffwys Ddraig*, but the generous window seat in the duchess's bedchamber suited her best. Set into a large bowed window overlooking the back terrace and gardens, it afforded her an incomparable view of the fields and hills beyond the estate grounds. With the casement window open, the night sounds slipped inside, a soothing symphony to her unquiet mind. The house held a man-made beauty not to be compared with any other home in the West Country. The land, however... The land gave her strength and purpose. Even under moonlight, it spoke to her.

Every field and forest had called to her, claimed her since she became mistress of the estate at the age of fourteen. From the morning after her hastily conducted marriage until the morning her father died, she had not altered a single piece of furniture nor changed out even one worn carpet.

"It is His Grace's house, my girl, no matter how long he stays away. I won't have him return and find it different from the way he left it."

Her father had been adamant in two things—the duke would one day return and bring her husband with him, and the duke would have no reason to question leaving his home in her care. The day after her father's funeral, Rhiannon had ordered the animal heads removed from the entrance hall, and she had not looked back. All of seventeen years old, she'd laid claim to the house and banished every vestige of darkness, brutality, and sorrow within those walls. By the time the old duke died, and she was duchess in name as well as deed, *Gorffwys Ddraig* was hers from the attics to the wine cellars. She fully intended it remain so.

"How went the dinner?" Beatrice Smith, Rhiannon's lady's maid, lifted the green gown from the bed and shook it out, inspecting it for stains.

"You tell me, Bea. The servants in this house know what I am about before I am about it."

"Now, Your Grace, there isn't a person serving you who isn't loyal to a fault," Bea admonished her. She stepped into the dressing room and returned moments later without the dress, but with a cotton night rail in her hands.

"Which means they carry no tales outside this house. Gossip amongst themselves, however, is perfectly acceptable."

Bea draped the night rail across a heavy brocade chair before the hearth. It was August, but *Gorffwys Ddraig* had ever been drafty no matter the improvements Rhiannon had made. The fire was just large enough to keep the room warm.

"Precisely, Your Grace. I understand His Grace left the dining room quite precipitously."

Unfolding herself from the window seat, Rhiannon swung

her braid over her shoulder. "You may His Grace *him* all you like. If you Your Grace *me* one more time when we are alone, you'll be leaving this room precipitously." She settled in the brocade chair.

Tall and slender, with white-blonde hair and cornflower blue eyes, Beatrice was a few years younger. They'd been friends from childhood. She'd come to Rhiannon over ten years ago, beaten and nearly dead. Once she healed, she'd asked for two things—a position in Rhiannon's household and her silence. Rhiannon kept so many secrets, her own, and Endymion's, and a few others she dared not contemplate—what was one more?

"We are not having this discussion again, *Your Grace*. I am your lady's maid and content to be so." Bea made herself busy preparing a cup of tea from the kettle on the fireside hob.

"You are my friend and the daughter of—"

"And you are avoiding the question," Bea said. She handed Rhiannon the cup of tea.

"What question was that?"

Bea rolled her eyes. "The one about this evening's dinner with your lost, but recently found, husband. The maids have declared him *criminal handsome and solidly built*. I told them those muscles are probably padding."

Rhiannon rolled her eyes and sipped her tea. She traced the pattern in the lovely Persian carpet with the toe of her mule. That was the question. She'd had dinner with Endymion and his friend for the sole purpose of learning why *His Grace* had suddenly traveled to Cornwall...beyond the reason stated in his ridiculous "invitation." Instead, she now had more questions than answers, and the sense her husband did, as well. Even the Marquess of Voil, whom her husband had introduced as his oldest friend, had been flummoxed by the duke's abrupt departure from the dining room.

"Was it something I said?"

"I am afraid so, my lord."

"I have never seen him like this, Your Grace. He is not himself."

"Then who is he, Lord Voil? You would know better than I. Who is my husband?"

"He is the man his grandfather has made him. But if ever a woman could unmake him, Your Grace, I do believe it is you."

"Does he need to be unmade?"

"Without a doubt."

Rhiannon did not want to unmake him. She wanted to discover why he had come, and how soon she might send him home. To London, for Cornwall was not his home. If tonight was any example, Cornwall would never be his home again. She refused to waste her sympathy on the man who had abandoned her like an old pair of boots.

She plunked her teacup onto the ottoman before the hearth. "Bea?"

Beatrice stepped back and shook her head. "I know that tone. And I know that look. It does not bode well for the Duke of Pendeen."

"My household is not prone to gossip. Is his?"

A flush of color dusted Bea's cheeks. Her eyes widened, and she put a finger to her lips. She scurried, no mean feat for a woman of her height, into the dressing room.

What the devil?

Rhiannon erupted from her chair. She strode to the dressing room door and peered inside to see Beatrice across the room pulling the door into the large bathing chamber closed. The maid turned the lock and removed the key. When she saw Rhiannon standing in the doorway, she put her finger to her lips once more. Then Rhiannon heard it, the sound that had her friend and maid in such a state. Male voices, faint, but definitely male. Bea shooed her into the bedchamber and followed closely behind her. She pulled that door to and locked it, as well. She handed Rhiannon the keys.

"They put him in the duke's chambers?" Rhiannon nearly shrieked.

"He is the duke," Beatrice hissed and tried to lead her away from the door.

"Of course, they did." Rhiannon threw up her hands. The thought of him on the other side of her dressing room set her feet in motion. She paced to her chamber door and back to the open window. Her mind raced, unable to hold a thought for more than a moment. "They set the table as if Prinny himself were coming to dine. Cook made all of his favorite foods."

"So I heard."

"She made orange pudding *and* trifle."

"Who?" Beatrice's face blurred as Rhiannon stormed by, but she didn't miss the ghost of a grin on the maid's face.

"Cook! Who do you think?" Rhiannon's voice rose, and then fell when Bea pointed at the closed dressing room door. "She has never once made orange pudding for me."

"Was she in charge of the kitchens when His Grace was—"

"No, actually. She started as a scullery maid in the old duke's day. She's only been in charge since my father died. That isn't the point," she snapped and immediately regretted it. It wasn't Bea's fault the servants had revolted or had taken leave of their senses. Or both. Rhiannon stopped in her tracks. "Who has he brought with him, Bea? Who came with him besides the marquess?"

Bea snorted. "Who didn't? His Grace brought his own footmen, grooms, a valet, and a man of business, to name a few."

"Good. I have a task for you," Rhiannon said as she crawled into bed and propped a few pillows behind her back.

"I'm not going to like this, am I?" Beatrice replied as she brought the night rail over to lay it across the foot of the bed.

"The valet and the man of business. What are their names?" Rhiannon retrieved her leather-bound journal from the bedside table, opened it, and plucked the stubby pencil from between its pages.

"The valet is Mr. Meeks. Appropriately named, as he hardly says a word. The man of business is Mr. Babcock. Vaughn has declared *him* to be quite full of himself."

Rhiannon smiled at her butler's assessment of Endymion's man of business. "Good. Start with them. I want to know why His Grace is really here and how long he plans to stay."

"You know why he is here. Lest you forget, I read that awful letter," Beatrice reminded her. "I always thought dukes were raised to at least pretend to be charming."

"Apparently, His Grace played truant from those lessons." Rhiannon made a few notes in her journal. "Find out what you can, Bea. I need to discover what provoked this sudden interest in the family seat after all these years."

With a last check of the bedchamber, Bea went to the door. "I will find out what I can," she said as she opened the door into the corridor. "But rumor has it his sudden interest is in you. Good night, Your Grace."

Rhiannon flung a pillow in the direction of Bea's fading laughter. In the sudden quiet, she listened for the sound of voices across the way but heard nothing. The case clock in her sitting room next door struck eleven. Perhaps he'd gone to bed. She looked at the keys where she'd placed them on the bedside table. Mrs. Davis, the housekeeper, kept all the spare keys on her chatelaine. Would she give them to the duke if he asked? Of course, she would. All he had to do was ask in that dark commanding voice and turn those green eyes on her and the woman would crumble like a Christmas biscuit.

"Oooh," Rhiannon screamed into her pillow and then punched it for good measure. "I don't care what Josiah says. There has to be a clause in English law that allows for a duchess to shoot a duke who deserves it."

How long she lay abed, never truly falling asleep, Rhiannon

did not know. However, she'd very nearly succumbed to exhaustion when a persistent noise in the corridor roused her. The embers of the fire offered enough light for her to find the candlestick on her bedside table.

Voices in the corridor, one she recognized and one she did not. Footsteps, back and forth, and whispered discussions. And then galloping? Something was galloping down the Turkey carpets of the second-floor corridor outside the ducal apartments?

"Oh, for goodness sake." Rhiannon padded to the hearth and lit her candle. She placed it on the mantle whilst she fetched her night rail from the foot of the bed and snatched it on over her nightgown. Almost as an afterthought, she plucked the keys from the bedside table and slipped them into the pocket of her night rail. "One night. One night in my house, and he robs the entire household of sleep."

Unfair of her?

Perhaps. The Duke of Pendeen was certainly responsible for her own inability to sleep, but he had been for quite some time before his return to *Gorffwys Ddraig*. She picked up the candlestick and stormed into the corridor.

Empty.

Not a soul in sight.

She peered into the darkness to her right, toward the duke's chambers. The doors into his bedchamber stood ajar. To her left, the corridor went past the door to her sitting room, past doors on either side to the family rooms—bedchambers and apartments long silent in disuse. The servants ensured they were clean and free of dust, but the rooms stood as empty testament to a man who drove one son to self-destruction and the wife and children of the other out of the house. A decision he later came to regret. If a man like him could feel regret. The late Duke of Pendeen had much to answer for, but she had guilt of her own to contemplate. Guilt might be pushed to the back of one's mind, but it could never be silenced. Not completely.

Rhiannon took a step closer to the heavily carved doors into the duke's rooms. A flicker of light drew her attention beyond the doors toward the stairs leading to the first floor. She debated whether to return to her own chamber.

"Hell and damnation," she muttered as she marched to those heavy oak doors and flung them wide. A swift perusal of the pretentiously large bedchamber revealed it to be unoccupied.

Where the devil is he?

The last thing she needed was a man she suspected of nefarious purposes wandering about the house in the middle of the night. Even if the law deemed that house his. Endymion had spent some of his early years at the family seat, until the old duke had made the biggest mistake of his life—a mistake that cost Rhiannon's husband everything. How much of *Gorffwys Ddraig* did he remember? What if he intended to breach her study?

"Oh no you don't." Rhiannon raced down the stairs to the first-floor landing. She nearly took the next flight to the ground floor, but a liveried figure at the far end of the wide first-floor corridor caught her attention. Once she traversed the thick green and ivory Aubusson halfway, she saw the man was dressed in the blue and gold livery of Endymion's London household.

"Where is His Grace?" she demanded once the footman saw her and offered her a bow.

"I am not certain, Your Grace."

Someone needed to teach the young man that if he sought to lie to a duchess, he would do well not to blush, tug his collar, and look at his feet. Worse, he would do even better not to glance nervously in the direction of the east wing.

Rhiannon smiled and started toward that portion of the house.

"His Grace does not wish to be disturbed... Your Grace." The footman wilted under what her household called her *duchess stare*. He returned to his position against the wall.

She should have taken the time to step into her mules. The marble floor in the portrait gallery would be cold. Somewhere, a mantel clock struck the hour. Endymion had left his chamber at four in the morning to visit the one place where she'd wrought the most changes in defiance of the old duke. Did he suspect? Had he been told? Or were his reasons for visiting the shrine to his much-vaunted ancestors something more personal? And painful.

Her candle flickered as she traveled the twists and turns that led to the long gallery in the Elizabethan part of the house. For six hundred years, each Duke of Pendeen had added to *Gorffwys Ddraig*, had left his mark on the house and the land. What mark would Endymion leave? It was no concern of hers. Just as his reasons for visiting the portrait gallery in the wee hours of the morning were not her concern. He was not her concern, save for the havoc he might wreak on her life whilst he remained in Cornwall.

Rhiannon turned the corner and entered the gallery. Her toes curled at the sudden imposition of the icy, gold-hued marble floor. Someone had pulled the heavy velvet drapes hung to keep sunlight from harming the portraits. Moonlight streamed in the long, mullioned windows and bathed the length of the gallery in an ethereal light. A lone figure stood before a portrait halfway down the long row of painted de Waryn ancestral memorials. A lamp had been turned up and placed on the marquetry table before the portrait. The arrangement of red roses glowed in the lamp's light.

"Oh, Dymi," Rhiannon whispered. She took a step forward. A shadow rose from the floor halfway between her and that lone figure. Near to the size of a Shetland pony, the shadow emitted a low, resonant growl. Its eyes gleamed in the darkness.

"I told you I did not wish to be disturbed."

She chose to ignore the huge mastiff that padded into a strip of moonlight a few feet away. "Then you should have stayed in London, *husband*."

A harsh bark of baritone laughter echoed down the gallery. "You may have the right of it, *wife*. Down, Turpin."

The mastiff subsided onto the floor, but watched Rhiannon as she went to join Endymion before the portrait she'd had hung the day she received the news of his grandfather's death.

"Turpin?" she inquired as she stood beside him.

"Being a male, I thought he might take offense at the name Black Bess." He continued to stare at the portrait. "I know what it is to have a cumbersome, inappropriate name."

"I happen to like your name...Dymi." He smelled of crisp, clean linen and a very expensive sandalwood soap. A long, black silk banyan was belted over his shirt, waistcoat, breeches, and boots. And here she stood in her nightclothes.

"It is good to hear you like something about me." He finally looked down at her. The smallest of smiles creased his lips. "I was beginning to wonder."

"I gave up wondering if you liked me three years after you left," Rhiannon said matter-of-factly. The chill of her feet crept up her body and lodged beneath her breasts. "About the time your uncle informed me you'd been deathly ill those first months and remembered little of your life before our marriage. *Burned away by fevers*, or so he said."

"I remember more than he or grandfather knew." He shook his head. "But less than I would like. Like a puzzle with pieces missing." He took a step closer to the marquetry table, raised the lamp, and fixed his gaze on the portrait. "The duke said he'd ordered this burned."

"He did." Rhiannon turned to take in the larger than life image—the handsome gentleman of thirty or so years standing beneath an ancient oak tree, his beautiful wife, from whom

Endymion had inherited his green eyes, dressed in white and seated on a bench, the gentleman's hand on her shoulder. Endymion, all of ten years old, with a grin on his face that spoke of mischief and adventure, stood behind his mother. That grin was embedded in so many of Rhiannon's childhood memories that it hurt to see it. Of the two other boys, the one next to Endymion favored their mother and the youngest, seated on the bench next to their mother, looked very much like their father.

The wind rattled the windows. The mastiff raised his head and whined briefly. Then silence settled in the broad space between the windows and the display of de Waryns past, but not forgotten. Rhiannon remained, because she could not do otherwise. As she had so many times in their youth and he had done so many times for her, she stood beside him whilst he sought answers for the unanswerable.

In this moment, he was not the Duke of Pendeen. At least, not the one who had written that ridiculous letter, not the one who'd confronted her in her study. Rhiannon allowed herself to compare this man to the fifteen-year-old boy she'd married in a hurried late-night ceremony neither of them had really understood.

The striking face and piercing green eyes had matured into the features of a stoic English lord, but the wild boy who had wandered the moors and ridden hell for leather down roads and across fields was still there. Shadows beneath his eyes belied the leashed control he'd evinced since his arrival. Taller and broader, he no longer had the lean and hungry look his childhood had honed from loss and a too early introduction to responsibility and blame.

He was handsome, dammit. Too handsome, too tall, too broad, and too much still the Endymion who had stolen and broken her heart. In spite of that lingering hurt, she slipped her hand into his. Her traitorous heart pounded like a miner's hammer when his fingers squeezed and held onto hers as if she might be the only barrier between him and the anguished waves of the past.

"It is my fault they are gone," Endymion finally said, his voice rough and raw.

"If that is how you remember it, your memory is wrong. There is a great deal of blame to go around, but none of it is yours." No one knew that better than she. And wrong as it was, she hoped he never remembered everyone who'd played a part in the dreadful night that took the last of Endymion's family from him.

"Who?" He gestured at the painting.

"Vaughn. He saved it after your father died and the duke ordered it burned. I had it moved here when your grandfather died."

He released her hand, picked up the lamp and with a sweeping gesture, invited her to return to the front of the gallery with him. The mastiff, his nails clicking on the floor, paced at Endymion's side.

"Thank you, by the way, for trying to distract Voil at dinner."

"Distract?" It came to her. "The Mermaid's Tale?"

"He doesn't know...about my mother or that part of my life." The strain of his voice, and that tinge of confusion and loss wiggled under her determination and threatened to awaken the silly young girl who'd been so infatuated with him she'd done all in her power to keep him safe. And all she'd done had cost them both.

"Lord Voil is your closest friend."

"He is."

"And yet you have not told him—"

"Madam, do you often wander about the house in your bare feet in the middle of the night?" Endymion plucked the candlestick from her hand and blew out the candle. He placed the lamp on the nearest hall table and turned it down low.

"What!" Before she could protest, he bent and scooped her into his arms. "Dymi, put me down. I am not a child."

He shifted her slightly against his chest. "A fact of which I am more aware every moment." He carried her out of the gallery and continued, in near darkness, down the corridors of the east wing.

She followed his gaze to her night rail agape enough to reveal her thin nightgown stretched taut across her breasts. "Is this an example of your wooing, Your Grace?"

"Do you want to be wooed?"

"Most decidedly not. Nor do I wish to be carried about in the dark. If you fall or run into a wall you will crush me, you great looby." Rhiannon squirmed against his hold. A mistake. His body was hard and warm, like a brick resting before the hearth for hours on end. She fought the desire to curl into him against the chill of the night air, against the chill of years of loneliness, responsibility, and the maintenance of a fiery dignity she sometimes had no desire to maintain.

Foolish woman, this is exactly the sort of self-pitying weakness a man like him looks for in a woman from whom he wants complete surrender.

"I spent the first ten years of my childhood in this house. I know these corridors as well as I know—Ouch! Dammit, what was that?"

"A Chippendale commode and a wall," Rhiannon offered and tried not to smile. He'd shielded her with his body, but she dared say he'd have a bruised arm in the morning. They passed the duke's footman in his place at the far end of the second-floor corridor. The man did not blink, gave no indication at all that the sight of the duke carrying the duchess through the house in the middle of the night was anything but a perfectly normal event.

Once they reached the door to her chamber, he allowed her body to slide slowly down his until her feet touched the floor.

"How is your arm?" she asked, her hands braced on his forearms.

"Apparently, His Grace's trophies are not the only things you have rearranged." He cupped her elbows and pulled her closer. "You needn't have wondered, Rhee. I have always liked you." His changeable green eyes ensnared her, fierce and gentle all at once.

"Dymi, please..."

"So much I was not allowed to speak of, so much I could not speak of because I could not trust my memory." He swallowed hard. "It made it easier, not talking about it. Not thinking of it. That's why I didn't tell Voil. About my mother or the rest of it. But I never forgot how much I like you."

"Lord Voil is your friend. I think he might understand." She resisted the urge to push his hair away from his face. She dared not touch him. He was a stranger and that was all he'd ever be if he had his way. He'd always liked her, but he'd left her here all alone to take care of the land and the people that should have been under his care.

"The past serves no purpose. Today is where life is lived. You know all of it, more, probably, than I do. Do you understand it, Rhee? Does any of it make a difference to you, at all?" He bent his head and brushed his lips across hers. He rested his forehead against hers and closed his eyes.

"No," she lied, and pushed up on her toes to answer his kiss with one of her own. He wrapped his arms around her and lifted her body against his. His lips were soft and cool, then hard and warm. Stars spattered behind her eyelids. She forgot to breathe.

What the hell was she doing? Rhiannon pushed against him. He released her at once. She took a deep breath and pushed her chamber door open. "Good night, Your Grace."

He tilted his head and studied her for a moment.

"Did you think one kiss was all the wooing I required?" she asked.

He rubbed the back of his neck. "I had hoped..." He was wise enough not to finish that sentiment.

"Your kissing skills have not improved that much, Dymi. Good night." She stepped into her bedchamber but leaned around the doorframe to watch him walk to his open chamber doors. The mastiff disappeared into the ducal bedchamber. Endymion stopped at the door and looked back at her.

"Neither have yours, Rhiannon, but I look forward to improving them whilst I am here." He raised his free hand and waved several keys dangling from his fingertips, a ghost of a smile on his lips.

Rhiannon patted the pocket of her night rail.

Damn!

CHAPTER 6

ENDYMION SQUINTED INTO THE SUN AND TRIED TO IGNORE Voil's diatribe against riding out *"before the break of day because His Grace cannot keep up with his duchess."* He tried to remember why he'd allowed the marquess to accompany him to Cornwall. Not a single logical reason came to mind. Frankly, logic and reason had been in short supply this past week. He had not set eyes on Rhiannon in nearly six days.

The house his grandfather had simply called Pendeen was a large and sprawling configuration of wings, orangeries, and gothic towers assembled over the centuries of deWaryn family occupation. Endymion had been prepared to present his case for the conception of an heir to his wife. He had not been prepared to have to search the entire house on a daily basis in the hope of coming across said wife.

She'd been playing least-in-sight since that first night. Since he'd fought the urge to kiss her and lost. Since he'd filched the keys to the doors between their chambers and spent the night wondering what she'd do should he make use of those keys.

"What did you say to make a woman like your duchess cry craven and avoid you like some pox-ridden old roué panting after her virtue?" Voil asked as they turned their horses up the wide road leading to the mineworks.

"A woman like my duchess?" Endymion tightened his hands on the reins enough to cause Dunsdon to toss his head in protest. He patted the big bay's neck and relaxed his grip.

"A hoyden of the first order."

"Her Grace is not a hoyden." Endymion tightened his jaw to quell a grin.

"She greeted us upon our arrival with one of Manton's finest fowling pieces on her arm," Voil reminded him. "Or is that something she reserves for wayward husbands?"

"Do you have a point, Voil, or is it your intention to simply annoy me to death?"

"Of course not. Being your friend has never been as much fun as it has been these past few weeks. And if you ever find yourself in the same room as your duchess, I daresay it will be vastly entertaining."

Entertaining. Not the word Endymion chose to describe a week of formal dinners with only Voil for company whilst Her Grace took a tray in her rooms or in her study. A study to which Endymion had not been allowed entrance since that first day. Nor was it entertaining to traipse about the house making inquiries of servants as to the duchess's location only to be told by the next servant *"You just missed her, Your Grace."*

His life had become a scavenger hunt in a house replete with half-remembered memories, none of them good. The only good memories he held of Cornwall featured a dark-haired girl who seemed determined to avoid him at all costs. He'd been taught long ago not to give anyone the power to dictate his feelings. Rhiannon Harvey de Waryn had done a damned fine job of establishing herself as dictator of his every mood these past few days. He might deny her ability to tie him in knots to the world, but he was not so foolish as to deny that damnable truth to himself. She didn't want to see him. The very idea bruised his...something.

"Good God, man, where have you brought me?"

The din and dust of the works settled across the road ahead, a wall of smoke, steam, voices, and toil. They rode up a hill into the noisome fog until it surrounded them. Voil covered his mouth and nose with his handkerchief. They skirted a deep drop-off edged with a railed fence until they came to a series of buildings. Several grizzled old men, mine workers, if their clothes were any indication, sat on stools surrounded by large baskets of rocks outside the closest structure. Endymion and Voil dismounted and walked toward them. The men slowly rose and removed their caps.

"Morning, Yer Grace," they mumbled as one and then bowed. They nodded at Voil. "My lord."

Endymion and Voil exchanged a look. Voil shrugged.

"His Grace has the look of the late duke," one bent, white-haired man said in answer to their unasked question. "'Cept for his eyes and his hair. Those you have from your lady mother, Your Grace, if you don't mind me sayin'."

"You knew my mother?" Endymion's chest tightened. He forced himself to breathe—in, out, in, out.

"Jim Digby, Yer Grace. Prettiest girl in three counties. Eliza Bryant, as was. She was a great lady." A few of the other men nodded in agreement.

Endymion cleared his throat. "Thank you, Digby." He briefly studied the other structures. "Her Grace was to have a meeting with the mines manager this morning. Might you know where I will find her?"

"Oh, aye," Digby said. "She's down t'mine with Mr. Thomas."

"Down?" Endymion walked to the fence and looked into the deep chasm excavated out of the hillside. Several mine openings were framed into the hill. "The duchess has gone into the mine?" He didn't wait for an answer.

With Voil shouting his name, Endymion ran along the fence to the gate at the top of the crudely cut stairs down to the mines. He vaulted over the gate and stumbled, slid, and slipped his way toward the bottom of the pit. His Hessians were not meant for such a descent. Poor Meeks would be in tears when he saw them.

Dammit!

His heart thundered against his ribs. His lungs squeezed against the invasion of the thickening air the closer to the bottom he descended. Once he reached the bottom step, he pushed his way into the cauldron of people, shaggy mine ponies, and bins of ore. The light at this level greyed as if in preparation for a storm. Voices—human and equine—fought to be heard above the *chinks* and *clangs* of the miners at work. His height afforded him an advantage, but to no avail. He twisted and turned, buffeted by the hive of activity. Still no sign of his wife.

What was she thinking? Mines were not fit places for the men who worked them, let alone a lady. She was the Duchess of Pendeen. She really had no business putting herself in such danger. She was his wife. She was Rhiannon. She was his to protect and the enormity of that task scared him to death. He'd succeeded at every endeavor he'd taken on since the day his grandfather had whisked him off to London and the life and duties of the heir to a duke. He'd succeed at keeping her safe, as well. As soon as he found the irritating, unpredictable—

A deep rumble drew his attention to one of the far mine entrances. A cloud of dust and debris belched out of the darkness. It suddenly came to him. His maternal grandfather had died in a mining accident. The ferment of people around him did not even look up.

He'd had enough. He had to find her. Endymion grabbed

the nearest man by the elbow. "Where is Her Grace?" he demanded.

"Whot?" The man cupped his ear.

"The Duchess of Pendeen. Where is she?"

"Aye. Herself is down Number Three with Mr. Thomas. Testing those new lamps of hers." He pointed to the entrance from which the noise and smoke had issued.

Endymion shoved his way past workers—men and women— and around ponies and crates of ore. They may not have noticed the din and cloud from the mine, but they noticed him. They stopped in their tracks, some doffing their caps, a mixture of deference and curiosity on their faces. Their faces all blurred together as if in a macabre dream. He threaded his way through them, his heart in his throat. The mining detritus on their clothes clung to the black superfine of his coat in ghostly sprays and puffs. He reached the mine in question and ducked beneath the timber-framed entrance. He swept his arm back and forth to dispel the lingering smoke. A woman of middling years, with a kerchief tied over her nose and mouth, led a sturdy red pony toward him.

In a slow sort of dance, the woman pointed down a tunnel to the left and executed a clumsy curtsy all while leading the pony toward the mine entrance. He ran past her. The clang and thud of hammers and pickaxes melded into a melodic drumbeat. He barely heard it over the beat of his heart. A group of grimy young men scrambled out of his way, muttering a chorus of *"Yer Grace's."*

Endymion, having shed all curiosity as to how these people knew who he was, raced in the direction the woman had pointed until he came upon a wide chamber, shored up by thick timbers at regular intervals. He came to a precipitous stop. In the middle of the chamber, dressed in a dull brown kerseymere dress and pelisse, stood his wife, covered in dust and perfectly at ease.

I'm going to kill her...right after I turn her over my knee.

A bandy-legged miner, hat in hand, argued with the duchess whilst an older man with a greying beard and dressed like a gentleman farmer looked on, some sort of lamp in his hand. "I don't like it, Yer Grace. It ain't natural. Not a thing wrong with the lamp I had," the man said, eyeing the lamp in the older man's hands as if it were a snake poised to bite.

"I'll tell you what isn't natural, George Watts." Rhiannon pushed a strand of hair off her face. "Blowing yourself and half your mates to kingdom come because you are too stubborn to try something new." She snatched the lamp from the bearded man and shoved it into the miner's chest. "Either you use the Davy's lamp or you can join your wife and mother-in-law at the calciners."

Torn between admiration and anger, Endymion stepped to his wife's side and, before she noticed his presence, dragged her arm through his. "Do as she says, George. You'll keep your wits longer. If this is settled, I'd like a word with you, madam."

Her eyes wide and her color high, Rhiannon tried to free her arm. "What are you doing here? I don't have time to entertain you, Your Grace. I have work to do."

Endymion caught the attention of the older, bearded man. He'd seen him in the foyer the day he'd arrived and again in the duchess's study. "Mister...?"

"Thomas, Your Grace. Josiah Thomas. I am Her Grace's mines manager."

"Her Grace's?" Endymion turned his gaze on Rhiannon, who met him with a fulminating glare of her own. "Then I am certain you can take care of this matter whilst I discuss a few things with Her Grace."

"Of course, Your Grace," Mr. Thomas replied and inclined his head. He appeared almost amused as he turned back to the recalcitrant miner.

Endymion started toward the mine entrance. Rhiannon

continued to try and wrest her arm free with as much subtle dignity as possible while he practically dragged her across the chamber and into the tunnel.

"I am not going anywhere with you," she said through gritted teeth.

Endymion bent his head close enough for his lips to brush her ear. "If you do not come with me this instant, I will throw you over my shoulder and carry you out of here by force."

"You would not dare."

He shrugged. "As you like." Endymion ducked down, pressed his shoulder into her belly and hoisted her over his shoulder.

"Dymi!" she shrieked. "Put me down. This is beneath my dignity and yours."

"So is digging one's duchess out from under a pile of rocks." He carried her out into the milling crowd of people gathered at the mine entrance.

"I'll show you a pile of rocks, you great bully. Stop this." She squirmed in an effort to dislodge his arm across the backs of her knees. Which gave him an enticing view of her lovely fundament. "Put me down and I will go with you."

"I don't trust you, Duchess. I think I'll keep you up here until we reach the horses, at least."

"Horses? I don't need a horse."

"It is a dashed long walk back to *Gorffwys Ddraig*."

"Not if I am slung across the shoulder of a pompous wretch like a sack of corn. People are staring, Dymi. Put me down, please."

He did not want to put her down. Here she was safe. So long as he touched her he could breathe. A sort of helplessness had consumed him as he wove in and out of the throngs of workers in search of Rhiannon. He'd known that helplessness before and every bit of his hatred of Cornwall and the weak young man he'd been was tied to it.

Endymion stopped and lowered Rhiannon gently to the ground. He studied her face, committed to memory the furious line of her mouth, the bright light of her eyes, the smudge of dirt on her cheek. And admitted, even if only to himself, something had broken loose in him, a shaft of light in the darkness he'd long given over to Cornwall and the past. The man in whose skin he'd lived every day, disturbed by nothing and no one, just as he'd been taught, had no idea how to live in a Cornwall no longer shrouded in darkness.

"What are you looking at?" Rhiannon asked softly, even as she nodded and smiled at the men and women eddying around them in a steady flow of industry and, yes, amusement.

"According to Voil, a hoyden of the first order."

"A hoyden?"

"The gun." Endymion adopted her agreeable smile and nod as she took the arm he offered and they made their way up the steps to the mine offices and storage sheds.

"Point taken. Why are you here?" She was tenacious, his duchess.

"I was under the impression the entire dukedom of Pendeen is mine to wander at will."

"You know what I mean, Your Grace."

"Perhaps I am here because my wife is so afraid of a simple conversation with me, she has gone to ground like a fox the last hour of a Boxing Day hunt."

"I was not aware that heirs might be conceived by conversation."

"It depends on how the conversation ends."

"*Tsk!* Good Lord, could this day grow any more tiresome? Captain Randolph, what brings you to the mines? Is there some disaster at the Swan and Crown?" Rhiannon slipped her arm free and walked toward the extravagantly dressed man conversing with Voil.

Tiresome?

Something about the man, this Captain Randolph, stirred a memory in Endymion. He had no time to think on it as he fully intended to force Rhiannon to answer his questions and to give him a chance to—

"Your Grace," Captain Randolph said and walked toward Endymion, hand outstretched. "Welcome to Pendeen."

The expression on Rhiannon's face lent him far more information than this man's bold assumptions and costly garments. Her opinion of the captain was even lower than that of her husband. A comforting thought. Endymion clasped his hands behind his back and stilled his face to his most bland expression.

"How kind of you to welcome me to my own home... Captain, is it?"

"Retired, Your Grace." Captain Randolph offered a negligible bow, his features frozen in counterfeit subornation. "Presently, I am the steward here at Pendeen."

"Steward? I sent for you the day after I arrived, Captain."

"Yes, Your Grace, I have been indisposed."

"Drunk," Rhiannon muttered under her breath. Endymion did not fail to miss the hardening of the captain's eyes nor Voil's bark of laughter.

A clash of querulous voices across from the mines office drew everyone's attention to a sort of rotating hearth before a monstrous furnace. A platform atop high scaffolding circled a large metal hopper. Several women with heavy kerchiefs across their noses and mouths were descending the platform in full cry at one another.

"I need to see to this," Rhiannon said and squeezed Endymion's upper arm. "Why don't you question Captain Randolph about the estate, Your Grace? I am certain he can tell you anything you wish to know."

The little minx. She'd put them both in their places and left the field in a flurry of kerseymere skirts.

"Voil." Endymion nodded after his determined wife. His friend gave him a look of resigned incredulity, but caught up to Rhiannon and offered her his arm. Which she took far more quickly than she had his.

"Tell me, Captain Randolph, how is it I have seen fields full of crops and sheep and what appears to be a thriving system of mines, yet the estate's income is in continuous decline?"

He only half listened as the steward tried in vain to answer his questions. Endymion had spent weeks in London going over the reports of the mines manager written in an uncompromising, obviously male hand, and the summaries of the estate's rents and production written in a hand very similar to that of his duchess. After three questions, the supposed steward's ignorance was clear. When Mr. Thomas joined them, the obsequious captain nearly wilted in relief. The fool put Endymion's queries to Mr. Thomas as if they were his own.

Endymion, however, had learned long ago to quickly ascertain a conversation bent on wasting his time. Something he found intolerable. His continuous attention to his wife as she soothed the riled tempers of several combative women whilst Voil looked on in tenuous consternation had nothing to do with Endymion's inattention to the empty droning of the captain and Mr. Thomas's impatient responses.

Rhiannon stood between two groups of women, silencing one with a mere gesture and listening to the other. She had their respect and, more important, their trust. She'd been left here, a mere girl of fourteen and had, somehow, grown into a duchess without the example Endymion had been fortunate enough to have.

The women dispersed, laughing as they strolled toward the pump just this side of the rail fence. Some chose to wash their faces and hands whilst others filled a bucket and made use of some tin cups hung along the fence to quench their thirst.

Rhiannon walked to the ladder that led up the scaffolding to the platform.

"Your Grace, I am certain you will agree that allowing children back into the mines will cut back on costs. Children work at half the pay of women and even less than half of what men are paid," Captain Randolph was saying.

Endymion turned to respond when the din was rent by a sharp crack and a shout. His feet were in motion even as he saw he'd be too late. The scaffolding and ladder collapsed, slowly in his mind, though he knew it to be an illusion. Screams, running feet, and the horrendous whoosh of crashing wood enveloped him.

His voice failed him. He reached the wreckage and began to fling broken planks behind him with a furious strength he forgot he owned. He had a vague notion of Mr. Thomas and some of the miners working at his side. They cleared a path and realized someone stood just the other side of the heap of broken scaffolding.

"Rhiannon," Endymion barked. "Voil! Where is my wife?"

"Pendeen, you owe me a new coat. This one is ruined," Voil complained from the far side of the rubble, his back to them. When he turned, Endymion saw Rhiannon, pressed against a retaining wall and shielded by Voil's body. Covered in splinters and dirt, the marquess attempted to tidy himself with his handkerchief.

All movement, all sound ceased as his friend escorted Rhiannon around the pile of debris. A wave of cold washed over Endymion and then a wave of heat. She barked orders at the miners and asked if anyone had been injured. Endymion clenched his fists to the point of pain. He could not breathe no matter how hard he tried. Finally, she saw him. She stopped, said something to Mr. Thomas, and then something to Voil, and then hurried to Endymion's side.

"Dymi?" she inquired as she touched his arm. He looked

down at her fingers, smudged with dirt. A few of her nails had broken. Her clothes were filthy and one of her sleeves had a long tear in it. Never had she looked so beautiful, nor so infuriating. And never had he been so lost from himself.

He reached for her, grabbed her upper arms and shook her. "Are you unhurt? What were you thinking? Why would you put yourself in such danger, you little fool?" He ran his hands over her, checking for blood or cuts or injuries.

She did not speak, only stared at him with doe-like, stricken eyes. She gripped his forearms and held on tight. Suddenly, every ounce of strength slid from his body. He rested his forehead against the soft cushion of her hair. Her breath wafted across his neck above his neckcloth and beneath his chin. He closed his eyes and listened to her breathe—softly, sweetly. Alive. He managed to match his breathing to hers.

His hands slid down to clasp hers. As if struck by lightning, his head shot up. He glanced around and spotted his horse. This time, when he dragged her across the dirt and rocks, she did not fight him. He lifted her onto Dunsdon's withers and flung himself into the saddle behind her. A chorus of questions launched at his back—from Voil, from Mr. Thomas, from the captain—pelted him and fell unanswered.

"Dymi, perhaps we should—"

"You will not put yourself in danger again, Duchess." He held onto but a sliver of civilized emotion. The Cornwall sky darkened. A vague rumble of thunder rolled across the valley. He urged his horse forward. He had to put the barren dust and caverns of the mines behind him. Trees, a piece of blue sky, a pasture of green beckoned him.

"You cannot come here and order me about like some lackey, Your Grace. I am—"

"You are my wife," he shouted. "You are mine to protect. Why the devil do you think I left you here? I thought you'd be safe. I was wrong." It struck him like a knife. "No more, Rhiannon. I will not lose one more thing to this Godforsaken place. I cannot. No more."

Too much. He'd said too much. Seen too much. Lost too much. Worse, the man he'd become had no idea how to make it right without losing himself. He'd never been afforded that luxury. If he shattered, how would he ever manage to put himself together again?

He'd lost his gloves. The tendons in his hands stood in stark relief to the white of his knuckles. Rhiannon covered his hands with her own. His strength seeped through the thin leather of her gloves and warmed her. The sky roiled, a dark grey kettle brewing a summer storm. Safe in the shelter of his arms, she watched the rain walk across the fields toward them. Even once it reached them, peppering them with stinging drops, Endymion kept his horse at a steady walk. She didn't mind. He needed the slow, dependable pace, the assuring rhythm of it. For the first time since his return, she knew what he needed from her. Even if she did not know why.

They rode on, down hedge-lined roads with verdant fields on either side. Save for the occasional drumbeat of thunder in the distance and the bleats of mama sheep calling to their lambs, no sound invaded the cloak of silence wrapped around them. Rhiannon blinked the rain from her lashes and tilted her head up to conduct a careful study of her husband's face.

Her husband.

She'd known the boy Endymion better than she'd known anyone in her life. She'd recognized the duke he'd become from the day of his return, a younger version of his grandfather, a man she'd in turns feared, respected, and eventually hated. Yes, she'd avoided him all week, but that did not mean she had not watched and listened and wondered. The previous Duke of Pendeen had manipulated lives, held them under his hand like chess pieces, and sacrificed them when necessary to secure the glory of the House of de Waryn. Upon his death, Rhiannon had vowed never again to relinquish her fate to another.

Today, she'd seen a completely different Endymion. Oh, the controlled and officious duke had been present in full force, but the man who'd stormed into the depths of the tin mine to drag her out of *danger* had infuriated and amused her. And, yes, revived the attraction she'd had for him all those years ago. The attraction that had led her to agree to a deal with the devil to make Endymion her husband. A pact for which he'd never forgive her.

"You do not allow children to work the mines," he suddenly said, his voice a pleasant rumble against her.

"No. They attend a school the rector and his wife have organized on the estate. In the afternoons, the older children work in the fields or on their families' farms."

"The lamps?"

"Davy's lamps. I read about them in a mining report from Wales and wrote to him. He sent me a quantity of them to test."

"Apparently, your letter writing skills are superior to mine." The bemusement in his eyes belied his expression, still strained and carved in solemnity.

She laughed softly.

"I should not have left my letter writing to my uncle."

"No." She held her breath.

"I...wanted to write to you, Rhee. I wasn't allowed. And then...it was easier not to because I didn't know what to say." He cleared his throat.

They'd ridden up the drive and arrived at the front portico of the house before she realized it. He dismounted and lifted her from the horse. She stared up at him, whilst a groom took the horse and Vaughn came out of the house exclaiming at the state of their appearance.

"It would not have mattered what you said, Dymi. It never did." She followed a still flustered Vaughn into the house. "His Grace and I are in desperate need of baths and tea, Vaughn."

"Of course, Your Grace. At once, Your Grace." The butler snapped orders at footmen and maids and started up the stairs.

"Vaughn," Endymion said.

"Yes, Your Grace?" He turned, head cocked in inquiry.

"The portrait." Endymion offered Rhiannon his arm. This time, she curled both hands around it.

"Yes, Your Grace?" Vaughn paled slightly and swallowed.

"Thank you." Her husband led her up the steps and past the smiling butler. When Endymion and Rhiannon finally reached the door to her chambers, he raised her hand to his lips. He turned it over and brushed his fingers across a scrape in her palm. His eyes never left her face as he pressed a kiss to her wound and closed her hand around it.

"I will...see you at dinner, Your Grace?" she asked as she gripped the handle on her chamber door.

"I look forward to it." He sketched a bow and started toward the doors to his own chamber, where his pale-faced valet awaited him. Suddenly, he stormed back to her, seized her in his arms and kissed her—long, hard, and with a passion that terrified her. "After which, you and I have things to discuss and you have questions to answer." He leaned in, his lips brushing her ear. "Like, when were you going to tell me someone has been trying to kill you?"

CHAPTER 7

SHE'D DONE IT DELIBERATELY, THE CLEVER MINX. ENDYMION refilled his brandy glass, leaned a hip against the black and gold chinoiserie sideboard, and watched. Watched as the exquisite beauty in bronze silk continued to charm and amuse the Marquess of Voil. Dressed in a shimmery gown that caressed her body like a lover, Rhiannon had entered the parlor before dinner and left Endymion and Voil in a state of attentive confusion, from the first sip of her before-dinner glass of sherry to the invitation to join her in the upstairs drawing room for brandy once the meal was done.

The entire meal had been orchestrated to ensure Endymion did not question her about the afternoon's accident at the mines, nor anything else of substance. An army of servants in severe black and white livery had attended the three of them. The devil, they'd outnumbered them four to one. Rhiannon knew full well that nothing of consequence was discussed in the presence of so many servants. She'd had her cook prepare ten courses. *Ten!* From the woman who had complained bitterly at the serving of four courses merely a week ago.

Almost from the moment they were seated at the table,

she'd engaged Voil in a lively discussion of the war against France, the social season in London, the location and management of his estates. And all the while, Endymion had sat, fevered and chilled in turns. Irritation crawled across his skin, a stinging centipede of awareness. He refused to lower himself to wonder why. He tapped the forefinger of his free hand atop his thigh. He dared not add to the conversation, for fear his first words might be...

"Where did you find such a dress?"

The fabric clung to every curve of her body. The bronze silk ebbed and flowed around her, a perpetual cascading fountain in the candlelight. It drew glints of every shade of golden brown from her hair. Hair dressed in an elaborate coiffure of curls atop her head, as elegant as any style worn by the loveliest of London's *ton* beauties. Her earrings and necklace were Whitby jet, glowing against her skin in magnificent simplicity.

To Endymion's mind, there was entirely too much bare skin against which the Whitby jet glowed. The gown bared her shoulders and a great deal of her chest in a bodice of crossed swaths of satin that lifted her breasts to the point he feared they might spill out for everyone to see. Well, Voil, at least. He took a sip of his brandy and scowled as Rhiannon's laughter flitted across the drawing room for the third time. The marquess was making her laugh simply to enjoy the effect it had on her bosom. *Bastard!*

"Did you say something, Your Grace?" Rhiannon inquired, her face a mask of polite boredom.

"Nothing of consequence, Duchess." He placed his glass on the sideboard and joined his wife and Voil at the arrangement of burgundy and gold damask settee and chairs before the fireplace. "Rather like our entire conversation at dinner."

"Are you saying I have no conversation, Pendeen?" Voil asked. "Doing it a bit brown for a man who barely said two words through ten courses."

"There was no need," Endymion replied. "You and my lady wife had all the conversation needed." He propped an arm atop the black marble mantel.

"Really, Dymi," Rhiannon chided. "What a ridiculous thing to say. Not to mention, rude."

"Not to worry, Your Grace," Voil said with a smile. "I am accustomed to His Grace's rudeness, being a victim of it on a daily basis." The marquess half reclined on the settee whilst Rhiannon sat in the comfortable chair next to it. Did the man ever simply *sit* on pieces of furniture?

"That is too bad of you, Your Grace. Lord Voil is a most amiable companion."

Endymion snorted. "He is a most pestiferous companion. There is not a settee, sofa, or chaise in my home that does not bear the imprint of Lord Voil's fundament."

Rhiannon's sultry laughter ran down Endymion's body like a caress. He barely stayed the involuntary shiver it evoked.

"If your house weren't the dullest establishment in London, I wouldn't choose to hide there so often." Voil, propped on one elbow, leaned toward Rhiannon. "I fear my virtue is in danger from so many determined ladies, I have no choice but to make myself scarce from time to time."

"Nearly every day," Endymion clarified. "Usually from just before luncheon until after dinner."

"Does His Grace truly keep such a dull house?" Rhiannon put her question to Voil, but she turned her teasing eyes, the color of Scottish whisky, on Endymion.

"I have attended Quaker funerals less dull," Voil drawled.

"I keep a French chef who is as fond of Lord Voil's handsome face as Voil is of Andre's cooking," Endymion replied.

"Andre?" she inquired of Voil, her eyes wide with faux innocence.

"What can I say?" Voil said with a shrug.

"If it is excitement you require," Endymion continued, "I

think we have come to the right place, if this afternoon's events at the mines are any example."

Rhiannon stilled. She swallowed and licked her lips. Her smile faded and then turned, brittle. "An accident, Your Grace. Surely there are accidents in London every day."

"Indeed, Pendeen. It was an unfortunate accident," Voil stated as he finally sat up. "The only harm done was to my coat."

"Accidents in London do not threaten the life of my wife. And three life-threatening occurrences in two months steps beyond the realm of accident into that of deliberate attempts to take my duchess's life."

Endymion levelled his gaze on her. She stared back, defiant. Angry even, and he repressed a smile.

Voil goggled, first at Endymion and then at the duchess.

"You have acquired a penchant for hysterics in the last seventeen years, Dymi," she said. "Not an attractive quality in a duke."

"I can assure you, Your Grace, Pendeen is many things, but he hasn't the passion for hysterics. He is the most practical, level-headed man I know." Voil looked from Rhiannon to Endymion and back again. "Would one of you care to enlighten me?"

She adjusted her skirts and rolled her eyes. "This conversation grows tedious."

"Two months ago, someone cut through every buckle on Her Grace's horse's bridle."

"Oh, for heaven's sake, I fell off my horse," Rhiannon started.

Endymion straightened and took a step toward her chair. "You fell off your horse whilst jumping a wall at the gallop riding sidesaddle, you little fool. You are fortunate to be alive, let alone to have escaped with only cuts and bruises." He was shouting. Not his way, at all. He moved one hand behind his back and squeezed a fist so tightly his fingernails sank into his palm.

This time it was Voil and Rhiannon's turn to stare.

"Josiah talks too much," she muttered.

"Not if it is true, Your Grace," Voil said, his tone uncharacteristically ominous. "Is it as he says? Was the bridle cut?"

"I don't know." She played with the silk folds of her gown. "It was an old bridle. Perhaps it was used by mistake."

Endymion and Voil exchanged a look.

"And what of your fall at the ruins, Rhee?" Endymion asked as he sat on the arm of her chair. "Was that a mistake?"

"Ruins? You have ruins, Pendeen? How quaint." Voil had a penchant for making light, especially when it might alleviate someone's pain.

Rhiannon's pain. Endymion saw it, sensed it. It drew him into the memory of her telling him of the death of his mother… telling him something, something his mind refused to allow him to remember, but just as frightening as what he was determined to make her admit.

"I tripped. The ruins are not safe."

"And yet you persist in visiting them," Endymion gentled his tone. He raised his hand toward her shoulder, bared by her gown. No. Too much temptation. He rested his palm on the back of her chair instead.

"When we were children, I might have said the same of you," she shot back.

"No one ever tried to push me from the battlements."

"I daresay, Her Grace may have considered it," Voil offered.

"More than once," she muttered. Rhiannon reached up to twist her hair. Impossible, as it had all been upswept, curled, and pinned into a ruthless work of art. Her hand slid down her neck. Her fingers caught her intricate jet necklace and toyed with the filigree gold. Of all the things to remember. She was nervous, afraid even, and it made it difficult for Endymion to breathe.

A primitive, soul-deep need rushed at him, a high tide of misty certainty. The where or the why escaped him. It simply... was. He wanted to keep her safe. Not because she was his wife, his responsibility, or even his duchess. The sight of her intending to twist her hair set up an ache in his chest. Keeping her safe made that aching need go away. It always had. If she was safe, she was happy. If Rhiannon was happy... She wasn't. Not now. Not since he'd arrived. He'd made her happy before, that much he remembered. He had, long ago.

"Are you listening at all, Pendeen?" Voil asked.

"Have you said anything of importance?" Endymion inquired. A surge of irritation and surprise drew him back to the present. Attention to even the most boring of conversations had ever been his grandfather's credo. One never knew when something useful might make its way into the bog of meaningless drivel that was polite conversation. As much as he wanted to learn everything about the woman Rhiannon had become, at this moment, he needed to discover what, if anything, she suspected about these accidents.

Voil threw up his hands. "I despair of you, Pendeen. I truly do. Her Grace assures me she knows the ruins too well to have ever been in danger. She merely lost her footing."

Endymion glanced down at her from his seat on the arm of her chair. She sat ramrod straight, her hands folded gracefully in her lap. The picture of a demure English lady. He suppressed the urge to snort. She met his gaze with one of her own—one that said *"Go to hell"* in English and Cornish, no less.

"Her Grace is correct concerning her knowledge of the ruins," Endymion said. "She has played among them since she was a child. Which begs the question, armed with such knowledge, what might cause her to slip and fall from a window in which she has sat and played princess thousands of times?"

His composed duchess used both hands to try and shove Endymion off the chair. He refused to budge, even when the heat of her touch against his hip and thigh set up a slow burn in danger of traveling to far more interested parts of his body.

"You played princess? How delightful," Voil said with a flash of his most charming smile. "No doubt, Pendeen here was one of many knights who rode to rescue you."

"Stubble it, Dymi," she ordered when Endymion opened his mouth to reply.

"Wait." Voil held up his hand imperiously. "You fell from a window? How did you fall from a window? Were you injured? When did this happen? Good Lord, Pendeen, why is it you insist upon keeping the pertinent details to yourself?"

"Finally caught up, have you? It is difficult to impart any details when one is forced to wedge them into the whirling dervish that is your discourse, Voil. And I only learned the details myself a few days ago."

"From my traitorous, garrulous footman," Rhiannon snapped as she exploded from her chair and paced across the room to the French windows that opened onto a balcony overlooking the back terrace. She spun to face them, arms crossed in such a fashion as to lift her breasts even higher in the damned dress. "Did you come all the way from London to put my servants through an inquisition, Your Grace?"

Endymion stood and took a step toward her. "If you mean, did I ask the footman who insisted upon accompanying you to the ruins and was swift enough and strong enough to catch you before you landed on the cobblestones of the old courtyard about your *slip* from the window, no, I did not question Tall William. He volunteered the information."

"I don't believe you," she replied.

She did. He heard it in her voice.

"Why would he tell you about something so trivial? Something that happened months ago?"

"Perhaps he understands that, as Duke of Pendeen, I am charged with the safety of everyone on this estate, especially the safety of my duchess."

"Too pompous by half," Voil—*When did he get up?*—muttered as he strolled past him, headed to the sideboard, empty glass in hand.

"You are charged. *You* are charged? Of all the arrogant, pompous— At what point, Your Grace, were you charged with the affairs of this estate?" Rhiannon stormed back to him, which, at least, removed her arms from beneath her bosom. "At what point in the last seventeen years have you bestirred yourself from London to even acknowledge the existence of Cornwall, let alone this estate?" Her face flushed, her eyes shone with righteous fury, and her hands fisted the glistening fabric of her skirts.

"Told you," Voil whispered as he ambled back from the sideboard and crossed in front of Endymion to hand Rhiannon a glass of brandy. The interfering rogue offered her his arm and escorted her back to her chair before the fire.

"It matters little how I acquired the information, madam. Suffice it to say, now I know, I intend to find out who is responsible and turn them over to the magistrate."

Voil stood behind the duchess's chair, a hand over his eyes, shaking his head.

"You *are* the magistrate, you daft..." Rhiannon caught the corner of her bottom lip in her teeth. His lady wife wanted to continue. Badly. She always chewed her lip when she had more to say.

Stubble it, you great daft looby. I am as intelligent as any man, Endymion de Waryn.

God help him, that is what he feared the most. She was far too clever. How had he forgotten it for even a moment? Each time his memory let slip another thing about her, about his life in this place, it startled and confused him. It lashed at his control, his one shield. His strength. He inhaled deeply. And looked away from Voil, who appeared to be having a seizure.

"Even better, Your Grace," Endymion started. "As magistrate, I can—"

"Was Pendeen the only knight who rode to your rescue, Your Grace?" Voil suddenly asked. He came around her chair and sat on the arm of it as Endymion had done.

"Was he…" She tilted her head to gaze at Endymion. A smile she borrowed from the girl she'd been slipped onto her lips. "No, he was not."

"I suspected as much. Surely, every lad in the county flocked to your tower window," Voil teased. He gave Endymion a pointed look. Unfortunately, Endymion had not the slightest inkling what the marquess intended to convey.

"Not so many as that, Lord Voil," Rhiannon assured him. "But there were a few."

"Aha! And who were these brave souls who dared to trespass on Pendeen's domain?"

Rhiannon swallowed. Endymion fixed his gaze on her delicate throat and then up to her chin, her mouth, her dainty nose. His eyes met hers. Dizziness, the sort one sank into when falling from a great height, blurred her face, but her eyes held him. Still he fell. Brick by brick, the wall he'd built against Cornwall crumbled beneath his feet. He was not this man. He was not.

"My brothers. We all played together as children. The ruins were our particular domain. We spent hours there, didn't we… Rhee?" He marveled at the steady tone of his voice. His face felt the same as ever it did. Composed. Dignified. Staid. With no indication of the numbness suffusing his limbs.

Rhiannon turned her attention to her brandy. She sipped it and studied the low flames in the hearth.

"Brothers?" Voil's bafflement was palpable. "You don't have brothers."

"No, I do not. Not anymore," his hoarse tone could not be helped. His throat had elected to close.

"What were their names?" Voil asked, his expression stricken.

Endymion raised his hand to rest it on the cool marble of the mantel. He'd heard the question. He knew the answer. And he knew if he opened his mouth to speak, not a word would escape.

"Hector and Achilles," Rhiannon said softly. "His Grace's father was a scholar of all things Greek."

Endymion steeled himself, drew the cloak of the Duke of Pendeen's consequence and reputation around him. He needed to move on, forward, anywhere save here. "As they cannot, you and I will have to serve as Her Grace's champions, Voil, if you are up to the task."

"I do not need even one champion, let alone two, Your Grace," Rhiannon assured him. "What I need is to be allowed to manage the estate without interference."

"As may be, but tomorrow you will accompany me on a picnic and a tour about the estate. Whilst Voil looks into the *accident* at the mines. You will not return to the pits."

Voil dropped his head and groaned.

Rhiannon. Rhiannon rose slowly. She patted Voil on the shoulder. She offered Endymion her half-drunk glass of brandy. Which, for some unfathomable reason, he took. Her expression was one of terrifying serenity.

"Lord Voil, you may do as you please tomorrow. As shall I. And you, Your Grace, may take your orders and your picnic and go to the devil." She quit the room in a swish of bronze silk. A log shifted in the fireplace. The ormolu clock ticked into the quiet.

Endymion downed the glass of brandy. It helped to reassemble the bits and pieces of his reserve she'd torn away in the last hour. Though the shredded remains of that much-vaunted reserve now fitted him ill and would perhaps never fit him again.

"Voil, I don't care what—"

"Stubble it, Pendeen." Voil stood and began to pace the thick wine and gold Aubusson carpet of the drawing room. "You are not allowed to speak. Probably not ever again."

"I beg your pardon. What the devil are you on about?" Endymion collapsed into the chair his wife had so hastily vacated.

"You. First, you acquire two brothers of which I've heard not a word in sixteen years. Then you order your duchess to attend a picnic."

"You said—"

"I said to invite her to show you the estate and to join you for a romantic picnic by the lake. Apparently, I should have provided you with a better definition of romance. It doesn't include ordering your wife about like a new recruit in the King's Navy."

"She's in danger, dammit. Someone is trying to murder her." He refused to explain to Voil the familiarity of the fear this threat evoked in him. It was visceral, made all the more so because he'd felt it before. At least, he thought he had.

"Who would want to murder your wife, Pendeen? We've been here over a week and it appears to me your people love her. Who would wish her harm?"

It came to Endymion in a rush of noise—horses, gunfire, men's shouts, and the cries of two young boys.

"The same people who murdered my brothers."

CHAPTER 8

"*THE SAME PEOPLE WHO MURDERED MY BROTHERS.*"

She had not intended to eavesdrop. Her intention was to make a dramatic exit and leave Endymion to stew in his arrogance. The extent of his meddling where he had no business had her ready to march him to the River Tamar at gunpoint. He'd corrupted her servants and made plans for her day with not even a pretense of consulting her.

And then he'd spoken of his brothers. His uncle had taken every opportunity to inform her *His Lordship*, and later *His Grace*, had few, if any, memories of his life before London. The fever Endymion had suffered for months after he left Cornwall had supposedly burned away his memories. Lord Richard had warned her never to speak of the past as it tended to upset *the poor boy*. Useless advice when she had not set eyes on her husband these seventeen years.

"Are you waiting for the door to open itself?" Bea asked.

Rhiannon started. Somehow, she'd traversed the corridors and stairs and now stood before the doors to the duchess's chambers. She tossed Bea a speaking look and marched through the duchess's sitting room into her bedchamber.

"The same people who murdered my brothers."

"He remembers Hector and Achilles, Bea," Rhiannon announced as the maid set about getting her out of the silk gown. "He remembers...what happened to them."

In the midst of unlacing the back of the gown, Bea's hands froze. "He...remembers?"

Rhiannon went over the conversation in the drawing room carefully in her mind. Endymion did all in his power to display no emotion, even when he spoke of the loss of his brothers. A strange thing she'd never considered. All people, even the strongest of men, showed their true feelings in little things, and these things often remained the same from childhood.

"His uncle told him they were murdered."

"Despicable man," Bea muttered as she resumed helping Rhiannon to undress. "There is something about Lord Richard I cannot like. I never have."

"There is a great deal about him I do not like, but now is not the time to confess those sentiments at large." She slipped out of the gown and handed it to Bea, who hurried into the dressing room to hang it up, to be inspected for stains in the morning. By the time Bea returned to the bedchamber, Rhiannon had rid herself of her stays, petticoat, and chemise and donned her sensible thick cotton nightgown.

Bea retrieved the flannel robe from the bed and handed it to Rhiannon, who promptly put it on and tied the belt in a loose bow.

"How did the plan to dazzle them into complacency fair?" Bea asked.

"You were correct about the gown. It worked quite well. Everything did until His Grace revealed someone in this household has been carrying tales, and then he insisted on using the tales to order me about like a servant."

"Carrying tales about?" Bea had an annoying habit of asking questions to which she already knew the answers.

Rhiannon rolled her eyes and sat before her vanity so Bea might help her take down her hair. "The accidents. The duke immediately came to the conclusion they are not accidents, at all. He believes them to be nefarious attempts on my life...by the same people who murdered his brothers."

"I see."

Not Bea's most helpful response.

Rhiannon looked over her shoulder to study the friend who had become her maid for reasons only Beatrice truly knew. She was born a lady, unlike Rhiannon, yet she unpinned and brushed out Rhiannon's hair with the intent efficiency of the most well-trained lady's maid. The most well-trained lady's maid with an entire regiment of secrets.

"What do you see?"

"Nothing I care to discuss, Your Grace. Save, I believe His Grace makes a great deal of sense."

"There is always a first time, I suppose."

"So, you agree? These accidents are not accidents at all?" Bea finished braiding Rhiannon's hair into one long braid and secured it with a bright red ribbon.

"Apparently, what I think is no longer important. Josiah Thomas and Tall William have seen fit to put the matter into His Grace's hands, as if I have not managed every situation to occur at Pendeen since my father died." Perhaps she should be grateful for Dymi's interest and assistance. Somewhere inside, she might well be. Overriding all of that was the galling fact his arrival had, in little over a week, usurped her role and made her feel...less. Like the girl who woke up the morning after her wedding to find herself abandoned, unnecessary. Nothing.

"Perhaps they are merely enlisting his help to keep you safe," Bea suggested.

"I have survived the last seventeen years without his assistance, no matter what the men in my service have decided." Rhiannon settled into her favorite chair before the fire and picked up the novel she'd left on the tapestry-worked footstool.

"I fear they have decided His Grace intends to stay. Until he has what he came for, at least," Bea said, eyebrows raised in knowing amusement.

"He is doomed to disappointment," Rhiannon declared and opened her book. "And now he will use his theory about these accidents as an excuse to take control of the estate and control of me."

"Control of you?" Bea snorted. "Poor man has no idea."

Rhiannon laughed. "No, he does not."

"If you have all you need, I'll bid you a good night, Your Grace," Bea said and turned to leave.

"Bea?" Through their entire conversation, Rhiannon had pondered her next request. A dangerous request, but one she dared not put off any longer. She only hoped... It did not matter what she hoped.

Beatrice stopped, hesitated, and then turned around. "Yes, Your Grace?"

"Find a way to send your friend a message. Tell him...tell him everything I have told you. About His Grace's suspicions, what he intends to do, and what he remembers. I would say tell him about what happened at the mines today, but I suspect he already knows."

"Are you certain?"

"No, but I want your friend to have this information. He will decide whether it makes any difference to his course or not."

"Yes, he will." Bea took a deep breath and let it out slowly. "I will see to it."

"Thank you, Bea."

"I hope you know what you are doing, Your Grace." Beatrice hurried from the room.

Rhiannon tucked her feet beneath her and dropped her book back onto the stool. "I hope so, too," she murmured.

∼

WAS IT THE CHILL OR THE DISTINCTLY UNCOMFORTABLE position of her head that awakened her? Rhiannon unfolded from the chair one limb at a time. A quick check of the mahogany bracket clock on the mantel revealed she'd dozed off hours ago. One minute she'd been staring into the flames of a warm fire in the hearth. The next, it was nearly three in the morning and the fire was mere embers.

She rubbed her hands together against the cold and shoveled several scoops of coal from the coal shuttle onto the glowing ashes. A few stirs of the poker and the fire burned high enough for her to warm her stiff arms and legs. If she were a better liar, she would tell herself she'd foregone her bed to read or simply to contemplate what she had to do tomorrow.

She'd fallen asleep going over Endymion's orders and suppositions, his determination to keep his confusion and sorrow from her, at which he'd failed, and from his friend, at which he'd most likely succeeded. Her last thoughts had been of her decision to communicate with...Bea's friend. She dared not even think his name at this point. So much was uncertain. Giving him information about her husband's intentions might place them all in danger. Rhiannon, most of all. Not a danger to her body, but a danger to her heart.

Then she heard it. The sound she had listened for until sleep took her. The door to the duke's bedchamber opened and closed. By the time she stumbled through her sitting room, boot-shod footsteps, accompanied by the pad of a large dog's feet, went past the doors to her chambers and faded down the corridor toward the back of the house. Rhiannon ran back to her bedchamber. She spun around in several circles in search of her grey woolen mules. They lay next to the bed, just where Bea had placed them.

"Good heavens," she muttered as she jammed her feet into them and ran back to crack one of the double doors leading from her sitting room into the corridor. She peered right and then left. The corridor was empty. A lamp on the marquetry hall table at one end of the Turkey carpet runners shone bright, illuminating the top of the stairs leading to the first floor. At the other end, Tall William stepped out of the shadows of the side corridor, another glowing lamp in hand. Rhiannon padded on nearly silent feet to join him.

"You told him about the ruins," she accused.

"Yes, Your Grace." The young footman hung his head.

"And Mr. Thomas told him about the bridle."

"I don't rightly know, Your Grace."

"William Waters, don't you lie to me." Rhiannon crossed her arms and patted her foot silently on the floor.

His face flushed. He swallowed once, twice. "He did, Your Grace, but—"

"I should turn you both out."

"Yes, Your Grace."

"Without a character."

"Yes, Your Grace."

She narrowed her eyes on his contrite expression.

"Or perhaps I should tell the upstairs maid I saw you walking out with the downstairs maid," she said with as much solemnity as she was able to muster.

He raised his head so quickly she heard the bones in his neck crack. His eyes widened, and his jaw dropped. Until he saw the smile she could not suppress.

"You are a hard woman, Your Grace, and no mistake," he said with a shake of his head.

"And you are a traitorous wretch," she replied as she took

the lamp he offered. "If you promise to shut your bone box around His Grace, you can keep your position."

"Don't let Mr. Thomas hear you use that language, Your Grace. He'll say it's not fit for the wife of a duke," Tall William declared.

"*Shut your bone box?* The duke is the one who taught me that one. Where is he tonight?"

Tall William tilted his head toward the hidden door set into the wall at the end of the corridor. The green and gold oriental silk wallcovering made the wall appear of one piece. One had to know where to press to open the inset door that revealed a narrow staircase to the nursery floor. The late duke, and all the dukes before him, no doubt, had no desire to be reminded they required servants to make their life of ease possible. Servants, like children, were to be seen, not heard. Until one had a use for them. No one knew that better than the current Duke of Pendeen. His grandfather had chosen to ignore Endymion's very existence for the first fifteen years of his life. Until he finally had no choice.

Rhiannon opened the door and made her way up the stairs, lamp in hand. She should have guessed he would visit the nursery after this evening's conversation. Every night since his arrival, Endymion had wandered the many corridors and rooms of *Gorffwys Ddraig*. She'd bridled at Josiah and Tall William speaking out of turn with her husband. She had no such compunction when it came to discovering what His Grace was about every minute of the day and night. The servants had reported his nocturnal wanderings to Mrs. Davis. And she had reported them to Rhiannon.

"Someone has to look out for the poor lad."

At the top of the stairs, a wide corridor ran the length of the entire wing of the house. This floor held the nursery, the schoolroom, chambers for a governess, tutors and nannies, and even bedchambers for the children too old for the nursery, but too young to be given a bedchamber on the second floor. The faint light from the first door to the left determined her destination.

His back to her, he stood before a large bookcase, hands clasped tightly behind him. He wore a long, black velvet robe, and she did not doubt he still wore his breeches, shirt, and waistcoat. He'd placed a lit branch of candles on the chess table before the window, a window with heavy curtains drawn against the cold. She knew, behind the curtains, the shutters had been closed, as well. Turpin had made himself comfortable on one of the three small beds in the room.

"My books are still here," he said without turning around. "And Hector's toy soldiers. We weren't allowed to take them when we left."

"You remember?"

He did turn then, his face drawn into taut lines and angles in the lamplight. "That we were tossed out of the house when my father died? Why wouldn't I remember? I was ten years old. We were each allowed one bag. Hector had to decide between his soldiers and Bertie."

"Bertie the Bear," she said softly. "A good choice for a boy of five."

"Indeed. I loaded my bag with books, but I could not take them all." He waved a hand at the bookcase, the top two shelves empty.

"You would have needed a trunk to take them all." She had stopped a few steps from the door, not certain what his mood might be.

"Two trunks, I should think. There were more books in the schoolroom, although I do not know if they are still there," he replied, a catch to his voice only she might notice.

"They are," she assured him. "I saw to it after Papa died."

"Ah." He did a slow perusal of the room. "Thank you."

"Don't thank me, Dymi. I only saw to the return of your things to these rooms once I was given full charge of Pendeen."

"From when we all played together. You always were the clever one. You remembered everything." He took a step closer.

"I remembered, but Vaughn is the one who saved it all after that dreadful Mrs. Stokes ordered it taken out and burned." Unable to stand still, Rhiannon strolled about the room. She ran her hand down the mane of Achilles's rocking horse.

"Mrs. Stokes was...housekeeper here," he said with a frown. "But I remember Mrs. Davis. She was here before my father died." She watched him search his memory.

"Mrs. Davis was a maid in the house when we were children. I offered her the position of housekeeper when Mrs. Stokes and I had our final dust up."

"Oh?" He sat down on the long leather ottoman before the fireplace. "When and why?"

She gave a short laugh and took a seat next to him on the ottoman. They'd often played this game as children. One of the four of them would have a grievance against someone. That person would name when and why the offense occurred, and the other three would pass judgement on the appropriate punishment.

"Papa would not allow me to change a thing after you and the duke decamped for London. Not a stick of furniture nor a single member of the household. Mrs. Stokes despised taking orders from Papa on behalf of *'that common slattern who calls herself a duchess,'* but she did so in the hope His Grace would return and toss me back into the gutter where I belonged."

Endymion's expression turned to stone, save for the faint tic at the corner of his mouth. "Your father should have flung her from the house the moment she made her sentiments known."

"I had Vaughn fling her from the house the morning of Papa's funeral. When I returned from the cemetery, Tall

William told me she had to be carried to the mail coach kicking and screaming. I wish I had seen it."

She and Dymi tried to maintain some solemnity, but, in the end, surrendered to a brief but satisfying bout of laughter.

"You attended your father's funeral," he said when their laughter finally subsided.

"There was no one else to go. I could not send him off alone." She had to know. He'd come to the nursery for a reason. And she did not want to talk about Papa's death and funeral. "Dymi, how much do you truly remember? You said it was very like a puzzle. How many pieces are you missing? It is just the two of us, and unlike my talkative mines manager and footman, I can keep a secret."

"I remember a great deal. I remembered Mrs. Stokes." He appeared to gather his dignity and demeanor as one might take a coat and gloves from a footman on the way out the door.

"Your uncle has taken great pains on more than one occasion to assure me you remember very little of your life before London and even less of me. You fell ill the day we married, were ill for months afterward, and the fevers burned it away. All of it. According to him, the entire first fifteen years of your life is gone. *Just as it should be.*" This last she delivered in a mock imitation of Lord Richard's overbearing tones.

"It appears you are not the only one surrounded by people who talk too much."

"What he said is true?" Rhiannon was half sorrowful for the years he'd lost and half hopeful, hopeful he would not remember everything about his mother, his brothers, and the circumstances of their marriage.

From the moment she'd entered the room, he'd held himself so stiff and upright, the perfectly postured duke. As if his height and build were not commanding enough. Slowly, he leaned forward and rested his forearms atop his thighs, his hands clasped between his knees. He looked across the room at the three beds, made up with quilts his mother had made. Rhiannon had visited these rooms from time to time over the last seventeen years. Each time, the weight of remembrance had weighed on her a little more. What must it be to experience all at once the good and the bad, the ghosts of a once happy childhood, cut short by banishment, poverty, and death?

"I remember next to nothing of the last year I was in Cornwall. Apparently, being in the throes of a high fever and being dosed with laudanum at every turn will do that to a man." He looked back at her with a grim half-smile.

Rhiannon's heart broke. "Oh, Dymi," she said softly.

"I have not spoken my brothers' names for seventeen years. I have done my utmost not to think of them, or Mama, or Papa or anything of Cornwall since the moment I realized I was in London and heir to the dukedom." He shrugged. "I told His Grace and my uncle I remembered nothing because it pleased them. I was a coward. And having an entire year swept away made it easier."

She slipped her arm through his and wrapped her hand around his biceps. As much as she could. What need did a duke have for such arms? He stilled and then reached awkwardly to cover her hand with his. The warmth of his touch seeped into her bones like sunlight.

"You weren't a coward. You were a child. They took you away from everything and everyone you'd ever known. They told you there was nothing for you in Cornwall—no family, nothing. And they offered you everything—London, a fortune, a title, Oxford."

His head came up sharply. "Oxford?"

"Your uncle. He made certain I knew you were far too sophisticated and educated a man to parade your ignorant country bride about the best homes in London. After all, you *did* take a first in Greek and another in mathematics."

"Did you not tell him you read, write, and speak Greek far better than he does? Far better than I do, for that matter."

"I did not see the point. I have learned over the years not to argue with Lord Richard."

"Hmm." He shook his head. "He was wrong about one thing."

"Heaven forfend! What could the infallible Lord Richard ever mistake?" Rhiannon asked, every word clothed in sarcasm. His dark chuckle vibrated against her body and turned her thoughts in an altogether dangerous direction.

"You, Rhee." He took her hand in his, raised it to his lips and kissed her knuckles. "He did tell me I had nothing in Cornwall, more than once, but he was wrong. There was always you." His green eyes held her transfixed. Clear, unflinching, and enticing as the devil.

"Dymi, please..." She was afraid, of so many things. The more time she spent with him the more of herself she lost. Or perhaps it was simply the more of him she found. More of the boy she'd always loved. More of the young man she'd married. He was so lost, and became more so every minute he spent in Cornwall. He just didn't know it.

"You were the one person they couldn't erase. Your name, I might speak. Your life, I might think on without pain. My uncle presented the estate reports as his, but I recognized your hand. You held all of my memories of Cornwall. You were alive, and well, and making my uncle's life a misery."

"I tried my best," she joked. Guilt swirled around her like fog on the moors. How could she tell him?

"I am not the most romantic of men, Rhee."

"You are doing fairly well so far," she muttered as she stared at their joined hands.

"The picnic was Voil's idea."

"I heard."

"Eavesdropping can land a lady in all sorts of trouble, Your Grace."

"You have no idea, Your Grace."

"Will you come, Rhee? Will you picnic with me tomorrow? Not because I ordered you to, but because you want to?" He used his free hand to tilt her head up. He touched his lips to her temple and then the corner of her mouth.

Rhiannon closed her eyes.

What now?

CHAPTER 9

Cook apparently believed Endymion intended to take Her Grace on an expedition to Scotland. He watched a young footman struggle to load the picnic basket onto the back of the handsome phaeton being prepared in front of the stables. Perhaps they should put a pair of the home farm's Shires into the traces instead of the sleek pair of matched bays.

Last night had been difficult for him. He'd revealed more than he'd intended. To garner her attention. To sneak beneath her defenses. Rhiannon was ever the champion of the wounded. The trouble was, his attempt to fool her had not fooled himself. For the first time since he'd arrived in Cornwall, he'd managed more than an hour's sleep. The fact he'd done so after his time with her in the nursery could not be denied.

He'd feared telling her the extent of his memory. Perhaps she'd think the things that had kept him sane all these years made him weak. He'd been taught never to share his thoughts and feelings with anyone. Ever.

A man who keeps his own council has all the wise advisor he needs.

Silence had served Endymion well, but it made for a damned lonely existence. Voil had been genuinely wounded he'd not told him of his brothers. The marquess had made light and chided Endymion good-humoredly, but he'd been hurt. Perhaps he should have told him. It might have prevented Endymion waxing maudlin with Rhiannon. Although—

"You persuaded her to go." Voil appeared out of nowhere to slap him on the back. "There is hope for you yet. Did you beg her, bribe her, or threaten her?"

"You are supposed to be on your way to the mines, Voil." Endymion pulled on his leather driving gloves and walked toward the front of the phaeton.

"I am on my way. I've come to fetch my horse, unless you prefer I walk all that way and ruin my boots as well as another coat."

"I prefer you discover all you can about yesterday's accident, and once you return here, I want you to find a way into the duchess's study and go over her ledgers."

"If this is the charm you exhibited last night, I am amazed the woman agreed to leave the house with you, let alone entertain the notion of a picnic. What did you do with her for nearly an hour in the middle of the night in the nursery, of all places?"

"That is none of your—"

"You need to get her into the bedchamber first, *then* you might have something to put in your nursery. Thank you, lad." Voil took the reins of the horse the stable boy had led out to him.

"I know how it works," Endymion said between clenched teeth as he gripped Voil's elbow and dragged him away from the stable entrance. "I was well on my way until Turpin had an attack of the winds so pungent, Her Grace and I had to flee for our lives."

"What?" Voil roared with laughter.

"Stubble it," Endymion ordered, perilously close to laughter himself.

"A word of advice, Your Grace. Next time you go courting, don't take the dog."

"She likes the dog."

"All fine and good, but does she like you?"

"I don't know." Endymion jammed his hands in his pockets and strolled back to the phaeton. Voil's boots rang on the cobblestones as he hurried to catch up.

"She cares a great deal for you, Pendeen. She frets over you rambling through the house at all hours. No other lady of our acquaintance would go wandering about in the middle of the night in search of a man she dislikes."

"So you say," Endymion replied. It came to him. "How do you know when and where I spoke with my wife?"

Voil offered one of his casual Gaelic shrugs. "She isn't the only one who worries."

Endymion threw up his hands. "Perhaps I should simply write it all down in my schedule book."

"Please tell me you did not bring that damned thing with you to court your wife," Voil said as he prepared to mount his horse. "If you have Babcock put a time and date in that damned book for you to tup your wife, I shall be forced to cut your acquaintance."

"Perhaps you should try it," Endymion suggested. "If you kept better track of which of your married paramours have angry husbands, and which widows are acquainted enough with each other to pitch jealous fits in the middle of a ballroom, you'd spend less time hiding in my house and eating my food."

"Good morning, gentlemen. What plot am I interrupting today?" Dressed in a striking military-styled, green carriage ensemble, Rhiannon marched across the stableyard from the side terrace of the house. A morning breeze sent loose tendrils of hair wisping across her face. If every general looked like his wife, Endymion had no doubt troops would follow her to the ends of the earth.

Voil cleared his throat and snapped his fingers in front of Endymion's face. "How the mighty have fallen," he said softly. "Don't muck this up." He swung up onto his horse. "You wound me, Your Grace," he called to Rhiannon. "Your husband and I do not plot. Does anything we do appear to be planned?"

"Idiot," Endymion muttered beneath his breath.

"Point taken, Lord Voil," Rhiannon said with a heart-stopping smile. "Where are you off to this morning?"

"I go to do my master's bidding," Voil quipped. "Enjoy your picnic, Your Grace."

"Ah, yes," Rhiannon replied as Endymion helped her into the phaeton. "The picnic you and my husband so carefully did not plan."

"I had nothing to do with it," Voil assured her. "I merely suggested it."

"Don't you have somewhere to go?" Endymion climbed up and sat on the bench next to Rhiannon. She smelled of honeysuckle and heather.

"I might have suggested the menu," Voil continued as he rode out ahead of them.

"Voil," Endymion warned.

"And told His Grace the perfect spot for a midday repast," the interfering fool called over his shoulder as he started up the drive.

"Do you have your Manton handy?" Endymion asked the laughing lady at his side.

"Josiah has informed me there is no clause in English law that allows for the shooting of a duke, even if he deserves it. I daresay the same applies for a marquess."

"On second thought, let us forget the Manton, shall we?"

"Are you afraid of me, Your Grace?" She adjusted her skirts and folded her hands daintily in her lap. The hoyden from his childhood had become a lady. For some unknown reason, he hoped the hoyden was still there, waiting for the right moment to appear.

"Always." He took up the reins. "Where shall we start?"

Endymion was afraid of her. Everything he'd ever believed about undertaking the business of the dukedom, she dismissed with her ebullient behavior and her completely unregimented day. They drove from tenant farm to tenant farm in no particular order. At some, she stayed mere moments, asked a few questions, and then moved on to the next. At others, she left the phaeton to inspect every nook and cranny of the farm and spent time listening to every complaint, great and small, whilst drinking some of the worst tea ever to leave China.

He walked beside her, acknowledging curtsies and bows, murmuring inanities, and coming to terms with all the things he'd lost by leaving her at Pendeen all these years. He was the duke, but she was their liege. Crops thrived. The home farm more than supplied the estate. The tenant farms were successful with no semblance of organization or direction he could discern.

She made him dizzy with her bouncing from one part of the estate to another. His uncle had told him Pendeen's decreasing returns were due to the duchess's mismanagement. Uncle Richard had declared her a flighty, scatterbrained woman with no head for business. He was right about one thing. Endymion was discovering Rhiannon did not have a head for business, but she had a heart for it. A heart for knowing her people, their strengths and weaknesses. A heart for Pendeen. Her love for the estate showed in the brightness of her eyes and the flush of her cheeks. She spoke of Pendeen as if it were a child and she its proud mother.

A child.

The one he'd never given her because it was not on his schedule.

"Do you intend to drive across the entire estate before luncheon, Dymi?"

She'd caught him ruminating. Endymion switched the reins to one hand and pulled his watch from his waistcoat pocket. His grandfather's pocket watch, which Rhiannon promptly snatched from his hand and removed from his person completely, fobs and all.

Endymion pulled the phaeton to a stop. "You took my watch, madam."

"Nothing escapes you, does it?" She dropped the watch inside the front of her dress. "You have checked this damned thing throughout the morning. I am not an item in your schedule book, Dymi. Nor are any of the people and places we have visited today."

"I am aware of that, Rhee." He turned the carriage down the narrow lane that led to the lake Voil had suggested as the perfect spot for a *romantic* picnic. Romantic. Endymion considered himself an educated man, but he knew not the first thing about romance. "Is there anything Voil has not discussed with you?"

She looked at him, puzzled for a moment. "The schedule book? He didn't have to tell me. Babcock lives and dies by it, and he fully intends you do the same. One of the maids moved it from one side of your desk to the other when she was dusting, and Mrs. Davis feared we would have to bury Babcock, he had such a fit."

Endymion forced himself to smile. Why was it so hard? At night when they were alone, she made it easy to smile. He'd played duke all day and dukes did not smile. Ever. He stopped the carriage beneath some trees at the lake's edge, tied off the brake, and jumped down to help Rhiannon. She placed her hands on his shoulders and allowed him to lift her to the ground. They stood, unmoving. His hands on her waist and hers on his shoulders.

"People and places are life, Dymi. You cannot capture them in little spaces on the pages of a book and expect them to do as you wish." She raised one hand and brushed her fingers across his jaw. "Life is a river, not a lake. Life flows in ways you never expect."

"Swimming in a river is far more dangerous than swimming in a lake." He touched his forehead to hers. "The things I cannot remember have been running over me like a river since I've returned to Cornwall. I need to keep some sense of order or I'll drown."

"Oh, Dymi," she said and pressed her fingers to his lips. "What did they do to you?"

Her dark eyes threatened to send him to his knees. No one had ever asked. No one dared. And he could not dare. He was the Duke of Pendeen. He was her husband and he did not want her to know what it had taken to make him who he was. The beatings. Days spent locked in a windowless attic room with neither food nor water. Threats, so very many threats unbearable to a fifteen-year-old boy. He straightened and took a step back.

"I hope you are famished, Your Grace." He offered her his arm. "If we do not do justice to Cook's feast, we shall never live it down." They retrieved the blanket from beneath the phaeton seat and wandered to a grassy elevated bank next to the lake. They opened the blanket and spread it in silence.

He was aware of her eyes on him as he went back to the phaeton to fetch the basket of food. He'd nearly given in to her questions. He didn't know a great deal about romance, but maudlin stories about his early years in London surely would not be conducive to wooing. He lifted the basket and carried it to the blanket. Once he set it down, Rhiannon opened it and began to arrange the various items between them. An uncomfortable silence joined them.

"Don't muck this up."

Damn!

"I don't really remember our wedding, Rhee," he blurted. "What was it like?"

RHIANNON DROPPED THE PASTY SHE'D FISHED OUT OF THE basket onto the blanket, missing completely the pewter plate in her hand. Their wedding? He wanted to know about their wedding?

She devoted her entire attention to retrieving the pasty and putting it on the plate. Of all the things to ask. Endymion sat down stiffly across from her. At least, his posture was stiff. She did not want to meet his gaze until she had a somewhat reasonable answer to his question. An answer she might give him without the guilt she'd carried for seventeen years being written all over her face.

"Is that plate for me or do you intend to simply hold it for the duration of our picnic?"

His question set her in motion. She offered him the plate and then pulled it back. He sat on the blanket as if seated in a London dining room. Legs out, perfectly aligned and back straight as if one of Chippendale's finest chairs supported him.

"Good Lord, Dymi," she said as she came up on her knees and placed the plate beside her. "Have you forgotten how to sit on a blanket?"

He scowled and reached for his plate. "I beg your pardon. *Oww!* What was that for?"

She'd slapped his hand. "For being a stick. Take off your coat."

"My coat?"

She grabbed the lapel and flipped it back and forth. "This coat."

"Why?"

"Oooh!" She huffed and reached for his buttons. The coat of

black superfine had been tailored to fit his form like a second skin. With a great deal of effort and entirely too much contact with his body, she wrestled him out of it and tossed it behind him. Next, she started on the buttons of his waistcoat, black with gold embroidery. At this point, he merely stared at her with an idiotic grin playing about his lips. For a man who hardly smiled, he'd perfected the art of the rakish grin.

"I don't know why I am surprised," she said as she removed his waistcoat and untied his neckcloth. "I daresay, you have not sat on the ground, let alone attended a picnic, since you left Cornwall. Now, that is much better." She handed him his plate.

"I'll have you know, I have attended any number of picnics in London." He bit into the pasty and closed his eyes. A reaction common to anyone who tried one of Cook's meat pasties.

"Dining *al fresco* involves tables and chairs and a battalion of servants. *That* is not a picnic," she said and went back to emptying the basket. Pasties, sandwiches, a jug of lemonade and one of ale, pickled eggs, strawberry tarts, and more. Cook fully intended His Grace not go hungry.

"And arranging our feast is not answering my question," he said, his green eyes studying her face as if it were a particularly difficult passage of Greek.

"Just as you did not answer mine," she replied and bit into a strawberry tart.

He did smile then, an honest endearment of a smile.

"What?" Rhiannon made use of the serviette Cook had packed. She wiped her mouth and nose, but saw no sign of strawberry stains.

"You always did eat your pudding first. Tell me about our wedding, Rhee. I truly want to know." He finished off the pasty and stretched full length on his side, his head propped on his elbow.

He'd remembered. A silly, small thing—her habit of eating dessert first. But he'd remembered, and it caught her off her guard. Enough not to push him to answer questions about what his grandfather and uncle had done to make him the sort of man who would make an appointment to beget an heir.

"We were married at *Gorffwys Ddraig* in your grandfather's study in the middle of the night. There isn't much else to tell." She took a delicate bite of the pasty on her own plate.

"Come now. All women dream of their wedding, or, at least, so I've been told. What did you wear?" He looked so ill at ease, she didn't know whether to laugh or cry. Even in the casual pose he'd chosen he looked awkward, and his grasping for questions made him appear even more so. Perhaps this was how it was to be between them. Flashes of their childhood friendship amidst long hours of the realization they'd lost each other along the way.

"I wore a blue walking dress. It had black stripes and black buttons." She broke off little pieces of the pasty and ate them between thoughts. "Vaughn gave me a posey of white roses from the conservatory and heather from the moors."

"Vaughn. What would we do without him?" Her husband selected a strawberry tart and took a bite. He chewed slowly and gazed at her from beneath hooded eyes. His lashes, long, dark lashes to make a woman weep with envy, swept down to lend a greater air of mystery to his expression "I am inordinately fond of the color blue."

"I know." She winced. The blue dress had been an intentional choice by her fourteen-year-old self. One of the few decisions she'd made that night for no other reason than to please him.

"And what did I wear?" he prodded. He eschewed the cups Cook had provided and drank some ale from the jug.

"A pair of your father's silk knee breeches, buckle shoes, frock coat, and shirt *covered* in lace. The entire ensemble smelled of lavender and the attics, fitted you ill, and itched you unmercifully. You scratched through the entire wedding." She refused to tell him of the remarks his grandfather's housekeeper made.

"Fleas, but what do you expect with that mother no better than she should be."

"Did we have a wedding breakfast, with some of these strawberry tarts perhaps?" He polished off the first one and reached for a second.

"Dymi, we were married by special license in the middle of the night the day after you lost your entire family. My father sent Josiah Thomas to drag the rector of St. Bart's from his bed to officiate. There was a horrible storm. The thunder shook the house. We were locked into the duchess's chambers for our wedding night, and by morning you, your grandfather, and nearly the entire household were gone. I woke up a marchioness and that horrid housekeeper told me if I wanted breakfast I needed to go downstairs and prepare it myself."

She wanted to kick herself. Her secrets were safe, the worst ones, at least. But in the space of a few sentences she'd revealed her hurt, her disappointment, and even her shame over their hasty wedding and its aftermath. He continued to eat his tart, which did not help, at all. The boy she married had worn his every emotion on his face and in his eyes. The man revealed little to nothing.

Suddenly, they both found the blanket fascinating. The breeze stirred the leaves in the oak tree overhead and sent little waves lapping against the shore of the lake. Ducks squabbled in the reeds along the far shore.

"Rhee?"

She sighed and, after a steeling moment, lifted her head.

"You were only fourteen years old," he said softly.

"It is ungentlemanly of you to mention a lady's age, Your Grace." She suspected where his thoughts had led him. "And you were a mere fifteen, Endymion de Waryn, though you considered yourself eons older and wiser than me."

"Did we... I mean, did I..." He cleared his throat. "Did we consummate the marriage?"

"Do you truly think your grandfather or even your uncle would have countenanced anything less? I know my father would not."

"I don't know which is worse, that it happened or that I cannot remember it."

"Don't you dare feel guilty. It wasn't awful, and it hardly took any time at all. Nothing to remember, truly." She'd never seen a man's face change colors so swiftly or so many times in such a short time.

He rolled onto his back and flung his arm across his eyes. "How can you even bear to look at me?"

"It wasn't your fault, Dymi. I suspect you were already ill with the fever that nearly killed you when they dragged you off to London the next morning."

"You are not helping."

Now she understood. Yes, he carried a great degree of guilt, but his male pride had also been injured.

"You were so ill you cast up your accounts immediately after we...you know."

He groaned and shook his head. "Have mercy, Rhiannon. Tell me I did not cast up my accounts in our wedding bed."

"Of course not," she replied, trying not to laugh. "You did so on my wedding dress on the floor."

He threw his hands into the air with a shout and then covered his eyes. The noise flushed a covey of grouse from some underbrush a distance away. The carriage horses threw up their heads and set their harnesses to jingling.

Rhiannon scooted over and sat on her knees next to his prone form. She tugged his hands away from his face. She ran her thumb across his bottom lip. His expression, a mixture of chagrin and apology, tugged at her heart. *Damn him!* For a man who supposedly had no idea how to court a woman, he was doing an excellent job of it.

"No wonder you did not accept my invitation to come to London," he said.

"I did not accept your invitation because it was rude, arrogant, pompous, and presumptuous."

"So Voil informed me. All the way from London."

"Perhaps I should marry Voil," she teased.

He lurched up from the blanket and rolled her beneath him so swiftly he took her breath away. His eyes shone emerald bright in the August sun. Beneath his fine lawn shirt, his muscles tightened. His body radiated heat of a sort she'd never experienced. Her blood flowed as languid lightning in her veins. She stood no chance to move, and to be honest, she had no desire to be anywhere save here, in his arms, for the next hundred years or so.

"I may not have done a good job of it, Duchess, but you are my wife, and I'll not share you with any man." Fierce and more primitive than she'd ever seen him—boy or man—he frightened her in every way she'd ever wanted to be frightened in all her most heated dreams.

"Why, Dymi? Why after all these years?"

"I have a great deal to make up to you, Rhiannon Harvey de Waryn. And I want to. God only knows why, but I want to."

He cradled her head in his hands and kissed her.

CHAPTER 10

WHAT WAS IT ABOUT HER? ENDYMION HAD CRAVED KISSING her since that first night in the portrait gallery at *Gorffwys Ddraig*. Every time he vowed to go gently. To woo her with soft, beckoning kisses. One touch of his lips to hers and every good intention fled. Her lips were so full and warm. He sank into their warmth and never wanted to leave.

She smiled against his mouth, the siren. She knew she held him trapped, helpless. The sweet moans she made as she met him kiss-for-kiss sent shivers down his chest and around his groin. Her hands brushed across his chest, brushing his nipples with erotic intention. She explored his upper arms and shoulders until she curled her arms around his back and sank her fingers into his hair, tugging the overlong strands down his neck, then massaging the base of his skull.

Endymion caught her bottom lip between his teeth and sucked slowly before sealing her mouth with his once more. He ran his tongue along the seam of her lips. She opened to him and teased the roof of his mouth before sucking him inside and slowly dancing around his tongue with hers. A force unlike any he'd ever known spilled from her into him and shook him to his core.

"Rhiannon," he gasped as he broke free to trail his lips along the velvety skin at the side of her neck. She shivered, and a bolt of pride and passion lanced through him. He rolled into a seated position and pulled her across his lap. Her dark eyes widened, pools of mystery set in a face flushed and aglow with a sheen of sweat from their exertions. He paused, one arm across her back and one hand already unbuttoning her gown. She hesitated only to hitch her breath and leaned up to press a kiss to his chin.

He struggled to undo the buttons down the front of her gown. She laughed, a husky, exotic sound that made his fingers stumble all the more. He splayed the bodice of her dress wide and set to work on her stays. They laced up the front, thank God, and he soon had them loosed only to discover the chemise beneath them.

"Did you wear this many damned clothes when we were young?" he complained as he worked to lift her breast from the confines of so many garments.

"There was no need," she replied. "I had no breasts. The rector's son said so. You broke his nose." She stared up at him, suddenly shy in spite of the palm she touched to his cheek.

"I'd break more than his nose if he were here right now." Perfection. Round and pert and topped with the most enticing dusky rose nipple he'd ever beheld. He ran his thumb over it simply to hear her gasp. His patience snapped and he bent to draw her nipple into his mouth to suckle, all the while torturing the tip with his tongue. Rhiannon fisted the hair at the back of his head to the point of pain as she held him to her. Every moan, every unrestrained cry hardened his cock all the more.

His free hand worked beneath her skirts. He dragged his fingertips along the silk stockings, the only thing shielding the sensitive flesh of her thighs from him. She opened her legs and allowed him passage to the heat his fingers sought. The coarse curls were damp and no match for his seeking hand. He pressed against her engorged flesh, pulsing in time to the rhythm he'd set at her breast. She moved against his palm, her cries growing more impassioned, more incoherent, until her back arched, and she flung her arms wide as she found her release. His heart thundered so, he wondered it did not burst from his chest. Spasms of sharp pains made it impossible to think or breathe.

Rhiannon fought to catch her breath. He rested his forehead against her breast and marveled at the rise and fall of her chest and the pounding of her heart against his skin. He curled his hands behind her back so she would not see how they trembled.

The breeze began to pick up. Dark clouds skittered across the sky. A storm was coming, but nothing compared to the storm at work in his heart and mind. Control, gone. Caution, gone. The strict, emotionless approach he'd always taken to physical relations, gone. His heart, as Rhiannon came to herself and gazed at him with a passion and something much deeper... His heart. Dear God, he did not know.

She attempted to set her clothes to rights. He pushed her hands away and did it for her, slowly and with great care. Whilst he concentrated on the task, he did not have to look at her. He couldn't. Every sensation, every thought was all so new and raw. She tapped two fingers to his chin and used them to slowly raise his head. He truly had no choice.

Endymion kissed her. He savored her lips, offered with a tenderness as foreign to him as a country he'd never visited, even in his dreams. She moved her lips in lingering caresses to the underside of his chin, the corners of his mouth, his nose, his eyes, his forehead. When she finished, she attempted to rise.

"What was that for?" he asked.

"For attempting to make up for our wedding night, of

course," she said with a saucy grin. She got to her feet, adjusted her clothes, and offered him her hand.

"Attempting? Good God, woman, it was one night. What is it going to take?"

"Seventeen years of nights like that might just do it."

He collapsed onto his back, arms outstretched, with a groan. She stood over him wearing such an odd, fey-like expression his limbs refused to work, had no desire to do so. Well, save for one particular portion of his anatomy. After what they'd just experienced, if that organ was no longer interested, they could bury him where he lay.

"What is it?" he asked.

"A memory. So much like my Dymi it... It doesn't matter." She shrugged and began to gather their picnic things.

He got to his knees and began to help her. "I am your Dymi, Rhee." His grandfather would brand him a sentimental fool in a world where sentiment destroyed men. More than the strength he gained from eschewing sentiment, he wanted her to understand he would try to find a way back to her.

Thunder rumbled toward them. The wind, heavy with the portends of rain, nearly whipped the blanket from her hands as she sought to fold it. The sky continued to darken. He took the blanket and snatched up the picnic basket, his waistcoat, and coat.

"Run, Your Grace, or you'll be drenched," he warned as he took her hand and ran for the phaeton.

"Afraid of a little rain, Your Grace?" She laughed as she ran, and it struck him they'd done this before—run hand-in-hand in the rain. He hoped so.

"No, I'm afraid of my valet. If I ruin one more coat, he will either weep for a week or leave without notice."

Endymion stowed the basket at the back of the carriage. He wrapped the blanket around Rhiannon. Drops of rain touched her upturned face. He used his thumbs to wipe away the drops. He studied her face.

"Mr. Meeks will kill us both if we don't return to *Gorffwys Ddraig* before the storm breaks," she reminded him.

"How could I have forgotten how beautiful you are?" He meant it. Everything about her defied description, his fierce and tender wife.

"The girl you married was not beautiful."

"Yes. She was. She has only grown more so since I left."

She shook her head. "Flattery will not gain you what you want, Your Grace."

Lightning lit the sky and came to ground on the far side of the lake. The ducks took flight. The horses began to shy. Rhiannon pulled away and started to climb into the phaeton. Endymion clasped her waist and lifted her up to the bench. He climbed up beside her and guided the horses to the road. They traveled in silence for a bit and he wondered what he'd done wrong. More important, what, if anything, had he done right? This courtship business had to be one of the greatest mysteries known to man.

He was the Duke of Pendeen, dammit. He was respected for the speeches he gave and the causes he supported in Parliament. He'd increased the wealth and holdings of the dukedom. He paid his bills in a timely fashion. He did not gamble nor drink to excess. He treated his servants with respect and paid them well. And none of it meant a damned thing to the woman who had been his duchess for seventeen years.

"Do you have a plan for this journey or are we simply going to ride until we reach the sea?" his wife inquired.

Endymion glanced around. The road was familiar. It was not the way they'd come, but he had traveled this road before and more than once. The rain had increased and the wind had grown fierce.

"We need to find a place to wait out the storm," he said. "The ruins are off the end of this lane, are they not?"

"We should go back to *Gorffwys Ddraig*," she insisted tersely. "They will be expecting us."

Lightning lit the nearly black sky. "They will be expecting us alive." He spotted the lone remaining tower ahead. "We are nearly there, and it will at least be dry."

She paled slightly and wrapped the blanket more tightly about her. The way to the ruins was an overgrown cartpath off the lane. Endymion allowed the horses to pick their way in spite of the cold rain and the ferocity of the storm. As the ruins grew closer, he found it difficult to breathe. The tower was intact, as was a large section of the bailey. The drawbridge, permanently down, crossed a moat now drained and dry. No one had lived in the castle since the restoration of Charles II to England's throne.

The wind had begun to howl and the rain came down in sheets, as it only did in Cornwall. Endymion drove the phaeton beneath a sheltered section of the bailey. He stepped down and secured the horses. Rhiannon sat on the bench like a statue, her eyes round and a bit wild. He came to her side of the phaeton and lifted her down. All the while, he sensed someone or something watching.

"Let us get inside the tower," he said and took Rhiannon by the hand. "It will be dry and perhaps we will find a fireplace that works." He led her across the bailey to an old wooden door, only half hanging. He pushed it and it fell back to reveal the narrow, worn steps that led up to the top of the tower. She stopped and refused to move forward.

"Dymi, I am not certain we need to do this." Rhiannon was afraid. He was not certain he ever remembered her being afraid.

"It will be fine, Rhee. We played here as children. I remember that much." He tightened his grip on her hand and led her up the stairs, higher and higher until they reached a landing that opened into a sort of great room. The wind blew so hard, portions of the flagstones were soaked. Across the way, a broken door listed to one side and revealed another room away from the glassless windows.

Lightning struck nearby, but did not fade. The room suddenly stood bright as day and every hair on the back of Endymion's neck stood tall and pricked into his flesh. He turned slowly and took in every inch of the chamber. His eyes fell where the landing touched the top of the stairs. Thunder filled the air in waves, an unending ocean of sound. Beneath it all, he heard his breath, harsh and short. His skin turned cold and his surroundings—sights, sounds, smells, the very room— began to recede like an outgoing tide. Somewhere, he heard Rhiannon calling his name.

His heart began to canter and then gallop in his chest. Voices came from the room behind the broken door. Familiar voices that breached a fog of pain, and fear, and the constant admonishment the past did not matter. Someone grabbed his arm and shook him. The clatter of horses crossing the drawbridge and filling the courtyard had him rushing to the window.

Nothing. The rain stung his face and still he could not find his way back to what was real. Shouting. Footsteps on the stairs. Gunfire. Screaming. And the storm. Above it all, the storm that never seemed to end. He'd hated storms as long as he could remember and suddenly he knew why.

"Hide! Into the oubliette. Hide! Don't come out until I come for you. I will come for you!"

"No, Dymi! Don't go out there!" Hands, young boys' hands clinging to him, dragging him back. He heard and felt his boots sliding across the slick flagstones.

"Dymi! Dymi!"

"Take him, Hector! Take him!" Pushing Achilles into his brother's arms.

"Run! Down the back stairs! Run and don't look back!" A girl's voice. Rhiannon?

"Stop shooting, you fools! The duke wants him alive! Go after the other two. Don't let them escape. Don't let them escape!" Men running. The sound of gunfire, farther and farther away into the night.

"Dymi! Dymi!"

"Where are they? Where are my brothers? Stop! Let me go! Let me go!"

"Let him go. Let him go! Stop it! Stop!"

"Dymi, please," Rhiannon pleaded.

His breath came in searing sobs. He rested his hands on his knees and shook his head over and over again. A gentle hand rubbed his back and murmured his name. The sounds began to form images, flashes in his mind. He remembered. Dear God, his brothers. He remembered.

"We were hiding here," he gasped. "My brothers and I."

"Yes," she said softly, trying to lead him toward the stairs.

"They came. They came and took me."

"Yes."

"I told my brothers to run and they went after them."

"Yes."

His throat drew so tightly closed it hurt to breathe, let alone speak. But speak he must. He needed to say it all out loud before it slipped away.

"They went after them and they killed them," his voice broke. "My mother was...dead. I was the only heir my grandfather had left and they came and took me."

"He offered a great deal of money to the man who delivered you to him. Only you, Dymi." Rhiannon, her voice in agony, threw her arms around him. "I'm so sorry. We should not have come here. We should not have come."

Endymion held onto her as if his life depended on it. He feared it might. All these years, bits and pieces of this memory had come to him. He'd dismissed them as wild imaginings, nightmares with no meaning. There was more. It beckoned to him, just out of reach, but he was so tired. His title, the money, the land, all of it had come to him, but at a terrible cost. Why?

"Why?"

"Because he could, Dymi. You were all he had left and the Duke of Pendeen never loses. Never." She clasped his head between her hands. "We'll go downstairs. We'll wait with the horses and then we'll go home. Please, Dymi. Come away." Her desperation cut through his sorrow and confusion. She'd been here that night and witnessed it all. He'd heard her voice. She was overwrought, and it was his duty to care for her. He could not help his brothers, but he could help her.

Together they made their way down the stairs. Endymion resisted the urge to look back. What purpose would it serve? But there was a purpose and he would find it. Right now, his purpose was to keep Rhiannon safe. It was enough. It had to be. He led her into the sheltered part of the bailey. The horses nickered in greeting. He found a narrow stone bench built into a niche in the wall. He sank onto it and pulled her onto his lap.

"You were here that night," he said after they'd sat in silence for a while.

"I brought food, and money, and blankets," she replied, her hands trembling as she stroked his hair. "You were going to leave for London in the morning."

"London?" His heart continued to race and his head spun as if wrapped in the menacing clouds just outside their shelter.

"It was the farthest place you knew away from the duke," her voice shook, and he hurt for the pain he'd forced her to relive.

"He was a ruthless man, Rhee, but I do not think he meant my brothers to die." In spite of his words, a heavy weight settled in the back of his mind. It did not help that she said not a word in reply. They sat that way, his arms around her and her hands moving over his hair and shoulders until the rain abated.

The sky remained grey, but the wind had died and the rain had moved out to sea.

They turned onto the drive to *Gorffwys Ddraig* before they spoke again. Rhiannon had grown more silent and withdrawn the closer they came to the house. As awful as it had been for him to remember, it had been even worse for her, or so it seemed.

"Why didn't you tell me?" he finally had to ask. "About the tower. About what happened there." Something about her reaction niggled at the back of his mind.

"I hoped you did not remember. And when it seemed you did not, I was relieved. I may be angry at you, Dymi, but I'd hoped you might be spared those memories. Even if it meant you forgot me."

He lifted her down from the phaeton and guided her around the grooms who rushed under the portico to see to the carriage. Vaughn met them at the door and immediately began to issue orders for hot baths to be drawn and tea to be prepared.

"I fear we look like a pair of drowned rats," Endymion murmured in Rhiannon's ear as Vaughn's orders set a beehive of activity in motion.

"Your flattery skills are lacking, Your Grace," she warned him.

They both were trying so hard to pretend the past few hours had not happened. To convince themselves they'd not shared such a horrific memory. He was shaken by it. She appeared terrified.

The servant they called Tall William came down the stairs and indicated he needed to speak to the duchess. Rhiannon gave Endymion's arm a squeeze and stepped away for the footman to attend her. Their conversation lasted but a moment. With a fulminating glare in Endymion's direction, she started down the corridor toward her study at a quick march, the footman close on her heels.

Vaughn was asking him something. A sudden thought made its way through Endymion's muddled and weary mind. He only made it halfway down the corridor. His wife stormed toward him, a red leather-bound ledger in her hand. Voil followed after her, more red ledgers in his hands and a panicked expression on his face.

Oh hell!

"You bastard," Rhiannon cried and flung the ledger into his chest. "It was all a lie. Take your country bride on a *romantic* picnic whilst your scapegrace henchman plunders my account books. I should have known!" Her face a mask of fury, her voice cut him more deeply than the sharpest blade. He'd hurt her, unforgivably so.

"Scapegrace?" Voil echoed, decidedly unhelpful.

Rhiannon stormed back to him and snatched the remaining ledgers from him.

"Lying!" She shied one at Endymion. He dodged it, just.

"Pompous!" Another, he batted away with his hand.

"Arrogant!" This one glanced off his shoulder and woke him from his stupor of guilt and surprise. He strode to her and stayed the last ledger, covering her drawn back hand with his own.

"I am not the one keeping two sets of books, Your Grace," he said quietly enough so the crowd of servants gathered behind him in the entrance hall might not hear.

Somewhere behind her, Voil groaned.

She stared up at him. Her body shook. Today, he'd seen her eyes bright with laughter, luminous in the throes of passion, awash with tears on his behalf. Now they were a dark void, unreadable and lifeless, save for flashes of something that struck at his chest like icy rain.

"Go back to London, Your Grace," she said and slammed the ledger into his chest. "There is nothing for you here." She walked around him toward the crowd of servants. Endymion caught her wrist.

"Rhiannon, please..."

"No!"

His head snapped back. His chin ached like the very devil.

She turned and walked away, shaking out the dainty hand that had delivered him a more than credible right jab.

Endymion took a step after her. Voil, one arm laden with ledgers, stopped him.

"I wouldn't do that just now, if I were you, Pendeen. I suspect duke season is about to open in Cornwall and, this time, both our tarrywags are in danger."

CHAPTER 11

Fool!

She'd always been a fool when it came to Endymion de Waryn. She'd joined in every perilous, reckless adventure he and his brothers embarked on simply to be in his company. At times, she'd subverted her superior competence in those things in which only boys or young men were expected to excel. Young men's pride being easily bruised.

Even in securing his hand in marriage, she'd gone against what she knew to be right, and she lived with the guilt of it every day. With him there—in Cornwall, walking the corridors and rooms of *Gorffwys Ddraig*—remembering the past, fear added to her guilt.

Rhiannon paced the confines of the duchess's sitting room. Her sodden clothes clung to her, a physical manifestation of the emotions broiling within her. Her feet squished uncomfortably in her half-boots and left damp marks on the thick blue and green Aubusson carpets. She'd had these rooms redone by Adam after her father's death. The furnishings were Chippendale, of cherrywood with silk upholstery. She loved her chambers, but now the pale blue walls closed in and made it hard to breathe.

He'd betrayed her. He'd sent his friend digging for information about her management of the estate. According to Tall William, His Grace was in search of money, money gone missing from the estate.

How dare he!

"Have you resolved to sleep in those clothes, or may I have them fill your bath and perhaps hold off for another day the pneumonia you intend to succumb to?" Beatrice Smith stood in the door between the sitting room and Rhiannon's bedchamber, slightly bemused, but greatly understanding of the madness to which an arrogant man might drive a woman.

"He remembered, Bea." The words came out in a rush, for Rhiannon had to talk to someone about the turmoil in her head. "He remembered what happened that night in the ruins when they took him." She fisted her hands in her soaked skirts.

The lady-turned-maid crossed the carpets and took Rhiannon by the hand. "What did he remember? Tell me whilst we do something about these clothes and your bath." She led her into the bedchamber where the copper hip bath sat before the fireplace, filled with steaming water.

"Why did you ask me about my bath when you'd already had it filled?" Rhiannon asked as she worked her way out of her wet carriage dress.

"One likes to allow one's employer the illusion of control from time to time," Bea said as she spread a large bath sheet and Rhiannon's heavy flannel robe over the screen. She helped the duchess out of her clothes and allowed her to settle into the comfort of the bath before she returned to their previous conversation.

"What precisely does His Grace remember?" Bea finally asked.

Rhiannon sank beneath the water long enough for the hot

water to warm her from the top of her head to the tips of her toes. Bea set to work washing her hair and waited. After a deep breath, Rhiannon related the events of Endymion's reaction to entering the tower for the first time since that fateful night. Her maid and friend listened in silence, punctuated from time to time by brief cessations in the washing and rinsing of Rhiannon's hair.

The silence continued when Rhiannon left her bath and sat before the fire wrapped in the bath sheet for Bea to brush out her hair. For the nonce at least, they each kept their peace about the duke's returning memory and all it implied. Once she'd completed the task, the maid helped Rhiannon into her robe and summoned the footmen to remove the bath. When they were alone again, they settled into chairs on opposite sides of the hearth.

"The marquess did go to the mines," Bea suddenly said. "He confirmed what I already knew. The hopper's collapse was no accident."

"How did you know?" Rhiannon tucked her feet beneath her in the chair.

Beatrice smiled sadly and tilted her head.

"Your friend?"

"He sent me word late last night."

"Yes, well, I suspect His Grace was not nearly as concerned about the attempt on my life as your friend. He took me away from the house on some silly excuse to allow Lord Voil to pilfer my ledgers. He suspects I am stealing money from the estate."

"Have you told him the truth? About the money? About your suspicions?"

"Of course not."

"Perhaps you should."

"If I knew of a certainty it was only Captain Randolph, I would, Bea. How can I tell him I also suspect his Uncle Richard may be involved?"

"You will have to tell him eventually, Rhiannon." Bea's slip in decorum only confirmed the maid's grasp of what was to come.

"It is all about to explode around us, Bea."

"It always was. You have merely done your best to delay what must happen. You've kept him safe all these years. Perhaps it is time he returned the favor."

"He will not see it that way."

Bea shrugged. "Make him see it."

Rhiannon gave a short, bitter laugh. "No one *makes* His Grace do anything."

"According to Lord Voil, you have made His Grace do a great many things in the few weeks since he arrived in Cornwall."

"He will never forgive me when it all comes to light. Between the secrets I've kept and what your friend is determined to discover, the truth may well destroy all of us. What then?"

"Unlike you, when it does, I can leave Cornwall," Bea said with a matter-of-fact sadness that spoke volumes.

"What about your friend?"

"He has more than proven he has no gift for forgiveness." Bea rose and brushed out her skirts. "He has sacrificed enough on my behalf." She pulled a folded parchment from the pocket of her brown kerseymere gown. "He sent you this. Perhaps, in light of what His Grace has already remembered, you may want to do as he suggests whilst the duke is still in your thrall."

"In my... Ohh, go to bed, Beatrice Smith." Rhiannon flung a small cushion at her friend's retreating back. She crumpled the piece of parchment and shoved it into the pocket of her robe. She didn't want to think about the threats on her life now. Not when the threat to her heart was far greater.

In her thrall?

A vivid image of his kiss, his hands on her body, his lips on her breast, suffused every nerve in her body with the shivery sensation of arousal. Her breath quickened. Her breasts grew heavy and sensitive. Not even in her darkest lonely nights, when erotic dreams of him in her bed were her only comfort, had she ever experienced what he'd given her under the Cornwall sky. Had the entire day been a heartless ruse? A way to keep her away from the house? A way to lower her guard so he might do as he pleased with no more care for her than he'd shown for seventeen years?

He'd married beneath himself; everyone said so. Her father had started as a mines manager in Yorkshire. When he died, he was the wealthiest mine owner in the north of England. His money could not buy his place in society, nor clean the soot of the mines from his hands, but it had bought his daughter the title of duchess and a husband of noble blood. His grandchildren would be heirs to a dukedom.

"Sorry, Papa," Rhiannon murmured. "I do not think noble grandchildren are in the cards." She drew up her knees, wrapped her arms around her legs and rested her cheek atop them. Her hair, nearly dry, fell around her face. She lifted the heavy locks and pushed them back over her shoulder.

From the corner of her eye, she caught sight of a rather singular visitor.

The large black mastiff padded around from behind her, a white handkerchief in his mouth.

"What on earth are you doing in here, Turpin?" she asked as she took the handkerchief from him and rubbed behind his ears.

"He is determining if it is safe," a deep voice replied from the vicinity of her dressing room.

Her heart caught and then broke into a clumsy canter. She clenched her hands until her nails dug into her palms. "It is certainly safe for him, Your Grace," she said when certain of the steadiness of her voice. She did not look behind her. She simply continued to rub an ecstatic Turpin's ears.

Her husband came around her chair and sat on the tea table in front of her. "And what of his master? Is he safe?" She could not help but notice he wore neither trousers nor shirt beneath his heavy blue brocade banyan. His hair was still damp from his bath.

"Don't you mean *my* master, Your Grace? As master of Pendeen, I suppose you are entitled to have your lackey break into my private study anytime you wish." She fought to keep the bitter edge from her tone.

"No man is your master, Rhee. I pity the one who tries." He took her hand between his. "And my *lackey* is cowering in his chamber in the hope of preserving his tarrywags from the wrath of the duchess's Manton."

Rhiannon had to laugh at the picture Endymion painted. Poor Lord Voil.

"I should have asked you," he said quietly as he ran his thumb across her knuckles.

"What?" She raised her head to afford him a full scrutiny.

"I should have asked you about the money, about why you keep two sets of books."

"But you didn't. You assumed I took the money or squandered it and used my accounting skill to hide the frivolous purchases of a silly woman."

"I... " He shook his head. "I forgot, Rhee. I forgot who you were, the kind of girl you were. Being here, being here with you has helped me to remember. If someone has tricked you or if the management of the estate ran away with you, tell me. I'll understand. I need to know where Pendeen's money has gone. I can help you find out."

The brief splash of warmth she'd experienced at his attempted apology disappeared like smoke doused with a bucket of iciest water. She snatched her hand free and flounced out of her chair. He had the audacity to appear surprised, affronted even, the great looby.

"Pendeen's money? *Your* money. You want to know what your country wife did with *your* money," she declared, standing in the middle of her bedchamber, arms akimbo.

"I didn't say—"

"Didn't you?" Her mind went blank and the leash she'd held on so much demeaning information about the dirty coal miner's *cit* daughter who had married so far above her station snapped. "You are sadly misinformed, Your Grace. Pendeen's money is *my* money. By the time your grandfather and my father arranged our marriage, your father's older brother had nearly bankrupted the dukedom with his gambling debts, breach of promise suits, and foolish investments. His Grace was in danger of losing everything not entailed. Surely you wondered why the duke allowed you to marry the daughter of a wealthy coal miner."

"I had no idea." He stood and took a step toward her. "I didn't know anything about the dukedom. I don't remember anything about our havey-cavey marriage, if you'll remember. I was half dead in borrowed clothes and I don't remember a damned thing."

"Count yourself fortunate, Your Grace. I remember every *havey-cavey* moment, including the one where you were so disgusted by your lowborn bride you cast up your accounts after bedding her." Every bit of hurt and shame she'd bottled up over the years came roiling to the surface. She needed to guard her words. She wasn't certain she had the ability to do so.

"You are hardly in a position to complain, madam," he snapped and stormed back to the door from whence he'd entered her bedchamber. He stood braced in the doorway, as if the door frame might keep him from coming after her. "Apparently, your father dangled your dowry under my grandfather's desperate nose and purchased my title and pedigree for you in the same fashion he would purchase a fine horse."

"Then my father was a poor shopper. The only portion of the horse I ended up with was the *arse*!"

A high-pitched whine filled the stunned silence that followed her words. Turpin stood between them, looking from Rhiannon to Endymion and back. He dropped onto the floor and rested his head between his paws with a heavy, put-upon sigh. Rhiannon opened her mouth to speak when she heard a deep rumble of laughter that sent strange tingles of anticipation to the most sensitive parts of her body.

Endymion was laughing, truly laughing, from the place deep inside where people so often hid who they were when no one was looking. She was looking. And hearing. And feeling. What had she said to evoke such utterly out-of-character behavior? He recovered quickly, though his face remained relaxed and an odd smile played about his lips.

"You and Voil are in agreement. He has informed me I am a horse's *arse* on more than one occasion."

"Recently?"

"About an hour ago."

"He is far more intelligent than I credited."

"For a lackey."

Rhiannon snorted. "For a lackey, yes."

"You are beautiful, Rhee, the most beautiful woman I have ever seen," he said, his eyes fixed on her in a way that made her stomach flip over and over again.

"Doing it too brown, Your Grace," she replied as he took several languid steps toward her. His feet and legs were bare beneath the banyan. He'd done it deliberately, damn him. He'd laughed at himself, the last thing she'd expected him to do. Then he'd made her head spin with flattery, flattery so sincere it almost made her believe him.

He stepped closer. So close, his feet touched hers and his breath stirred her hair. He gathered a handful of her thick, dark curls, raised them to his face and inhaled, then rubbed the locks against his cheek. The sharply drawn lines of his face stood in stark contrast to the gentle whirls of her hair. His expression was taut, as if some unseen current lurked beneath his skin. She wanted to be afraid or even angry, but her foolish body refused to cooperate. He was tall and broad and powerful, and far too male to be denied. And, God help her, she did not want to deny him.

"You always had the sweetest hair, Rhee. All these curls, and soft as a feather bed." He touched the backs of his fingers to her temple and glided down her neck to the place where her collarbone peeked through her robe.

"What do you want, Dymi?" Rhiannon mentally scrambled away from the cliff's edge that was her husband's eyes lit with passion, his touch warm with desire. One misstep and she'd tumble over, and the landing could be her undoing.

"You, Rhee. Other than that, I haven't the merest clue as to what I want. What *I* want. Not the Duke of Pendeen. Not the man who is trying desperately to hold to the little bit of control he has left for fear he cannot exist without it." He caressed her shoulders, slid down her arms until he held her hands in his. "I'm so weary, and I don't know why. I only know with you...in bits and pieces...I can become someone other than the man I have had to be these seventeen years."

"Why me? I am nothing to you, Dymi."

"You are the *only* thing to me. I am a stranger here. Nothing speaks to me. Flashes of memory, all horrible and mixed up and lonely. You are the only true thing I have left here. You are the only rest I have found in Cornwall." His hands tightened around hers, as if she were a lifeline thrown to him in a stormy sea. "After this afternoon, I...I... I am rubbish at this, Rhee. I don't know what to say or how to tell you how much I want to find my way back to you. Or even why. I just—"

The rigid, uncompromising duke was gone. In his place stood the man who'd dared everything to take care of his mother and brothers. The man who'd gone where passion led him, and she wanted passion to lead him now.

"Stop talking and kiss me, you horse's *arse*." Rhiannon fisted the lapels of his banyan and dragged him against her. Fortunately, His Grace did not have to be told twice.

He seized her beneath her elbows and crushed her in an embrace so powerful it took her breath away. His lips took hers in a fiery kiss, his groan so deep and dark it forced her to release his robe and curl her arms around his neck for dear life. His hands moved from her elbows around her back and wrapped themselves in her hair.

He caught her top lip between his teeth, tugged gently and then suckled it. Then his lips burned a path of kisses and nips across her chin and down her throat to the vee bared by her robe. With one muscled arm around her, he lifted her feet from the floor and, with the other hand, loosen the tie of her robe.

Rhiannon ran her tongue around his ear and bit the lobe sharply. He flinched, groaned, and held her tighter. She reveled in the silk of his hair, its length a reminder of the wild boy she'd fallen in love with at first sight. *Love?* Oh no, this had nothing to do with love. He'd awakened a sleeping passion in her under the trees by the lake. She was no simpering lady. She loved the wicked sensations, the completely improper hunger his body unleashed in hers, and she wanted more. She held no hope he'd suddenly become the husband she'd dreamed of, but for now, she'd take the husband he'd decided to be. Whoever he was.

Liar! Foolish, foolish, girl!

Her eyes met his, and then they both lowered their gaze. He'd lifted her breast from her gapped robe and held it reverently. He pressed a kiss to the curved mound, whispering his lips across the edge of her tightly furled nipple.

"Tell me no, Rhiannon," he spoke against her sensitized skin. "Send me away. It will break my heart, but I will go."

She traced a path along his neck, down his chest and inside

the confines of his banyan until her fingertip found the hardened length jutting against the silk folds of that garment. She bent her head to kiss the back of his neck and then touched her mouth to his ear. "It will break something, Your Grace, but I daresay it is not your heart."

He raised his head and curled his fingers around her breast. "You are a wicked, cruel woman, Duchess," he rasped, then kissed her until she lost the ability to draw breath, to think, or to admit what a truly bad decision she was about to make. She'd lived the last seventeen years for Pendeen. Tonight, she'd live for herself, and tomorrow she'd do what she did best—pick up the pieces and carry on without him.

"Take a wicked duchess to bed, Your Grace?" She tugged the tie of his banyan free.

He stared at her, ferocious possession simmering beneath every dignified line of restraint. "You scare the devil out of me, Rhiannon de Waryn, and I'll take you to bed until you beg me to stop."

Backing to the bed, they wrestled her out of her clothes. Endymion dropped them onto the counterpane, wrapped his hands around her waist, and tossed her onto the bed. She lay there, propped on her elbows, and watched him throw aside the quilted banyan. This was no idle London lord. Broad, strong shoulders tapered down into the sinewed arms that had held her so fiercely she scarcely wanted to leave. His chest, sculpted flesh to make a Roman statue weep, sported a light dusting of dark hair leading down to a flat stomach, thick horseman's thighs and...she didn't remember him being built quite so solidly...there.

"My Cornwall beauty, wife," he murmured.

She scooted back across the bed. A slow smile curved his lips. He wrapped his fingers around one ankle and held her there as he propped a knee on the bed and crawled to her. Once his face drew even with hers, he released her ankle and used undulating brushes of his chest and thighs to keep her in place. Her body sang with excitement—spinning wheels of fire and ice in her veins, up and down her flesh. She had no strength for escape.

Endymion kissed her, a chaste press of his lips to her forehead, another to the tip of her nose, another to her chin. He worked his way down her body with more frustrating, brief kisses to her chest, the tips of her breasts, her navel, and to the tangle of curls where her thighs met. He covered her knees with his long fingers, urged them apart, and pressed a far more heated kiss to a place she'd never dreamed of being kissed.

"What are you—" The rest was lost in a series of incoherent cries over which Rhiannon had no control. He tortured her damp, swollen flesh with his tongue—flicking, swirling, licking, pressing, and holding his tongue against the seat of her pleasure. She tried to move her legs, closer or farther apart, it did not matter. She needed to move. And when she finally did, it was to lift herself into his attentions, pulsing until the rhythm began to give her what she sought. He was merciless, chuckling at her moans and pleading. Growling against her screaming flesh until her body reached for completion, found it, and dragged her into the undertow he'd set loose.

She called his name, and before her soul returned to her body, he was over her, his mouth at her breast as he slid himself inside her in one slow, stretching, filling slide. She clutched the back of his head, holding him to her as he suckled and matched his thrusts to her desperate rhythm. The sense of fullness was strange at first. It had been seventeen years and only the one time. This was nothing like before, and she found herself wanting more, wanting it never to end.

Endymion rose on his arms. His rhythm quickened. He lowered his head to kiss her, and suddenly Rhiannon had to strive with him, against him. The spiral of pleasure began to whirl around her once more. The sounds of their flesh meeting, his dark groans, her panting cries—all of it began to spin out of control. His gaze locked with hers. She gripped his forearms for fear she'd fly away into the green forest of his eyes.

"Rhiannon," he breathed. "Rhiannon." Over and over, he gasped her name, until he had no breath left to speak. His eyes closed, his expression one of feral concentration.

Suddenly her vision went dark and then exploded with colors and light. Her body locked. He threw his head back, an incomprehensible groan exploding from his lips. His arms shook slightly, but still held him above her. She pulled him down, needing the heat he radiated, needing the sense of his flesh against hers to assure her this wasn't all a dream. She wrapped her arms around him. Kissed the damp hair away from his face.

He pressed an awkward kiss to her cheek and nuzzled his face into the cloud of her hair spread across the bedclothes. He sighed and then chuckled a moment.

"Why are you laughing?"

"My *arse* is freezing, but I don't want to move."

"We can wait a few moments to find our way under the covers." She stroked his back and began to wonder how she had allowed this to happen.

"I don't want to move, ever."

"That may prove problematic. I have things to see to in the morning." Rhiannon winced at the casual tone she'd adopted. It was the most incredible moment of her life, but she did not want him to know it. She could not give him that power. She'd already given in to him. A mere two weeks, and she'd fallen into his bed.

He raised himself up once more. "Are you angry with me, Rhee? Did I hurt you?" He truly was concerned, which made it all the worse.

"Of course, you didn't, you stupid man. It was wonderful. I never knew— Stop smiling at me."

"It isn't every day a man beds his wife for the first time he remembers and she tells him he is wonderful." He kissed her nose. She batted him away.

"Oh, for goodness sake." She scrambled from beneath him and worked her way under the sheets and counterpane at the head of the bed. He propped himself up on one elbow and fixed her with an inquiring stare. She flipped the covers back from the spot on the bed beside her.

"Are you certain, Rhee? You seem a bit upset for a woman who has been *wonderfully* pleasured. Lord Voil isn't the only one who values his tarrywags."

She rolled her eyes. She wanted to be furious with him. She needed to be. But all she craved was the warmth and weight of his body next to hers as she drifted to sleep. Even if he'd return to London once August ended. She'd survived it as a girl. She expected she'd survive it again. She had no choice.

"You do have a rather fine *arse*, Your Grace. I'd hate to see it damaged by frostbite."

He made a great show of leaving the bed, walking to the spot she'd indicated, and climbing back in again. He stretched out beside her and pulled her close as he settled the sheets and counterpane over them.

"I am curious about one thing, Dymi."

"Ask me anything, Rhee." He kissed her hair, which he took great care to spread across his chest.

"With a wife tucked away in Cornwall since you were fifteen, where precisely did you learn to perform so wonderfully in bed?"

CHAPTER 12

Why could I not have married a placid wife of average wit with a complete lack of curiosity?

Endymion wistfully considered that fleeting thought whilst he tried to compose an answer for the far too quick-witted woman he'd married. An answer that would not undo the entirety of his inept wooing. At least, he hoped his wooing had persuaded her to take him into her bed.

He could always tell her the truth. The late duke would, no doubt, turn over in his grave.

"Women do not need the truth. They need to hear whatever gives them comfort. It is all they want or understand."

She turned on her side and stared at him expectantly. They occupied her bedchamber. Where did she keep her Manton? He braced himself.

"My grandfather—ompff! What the devil?" His head had gone fuzzy. His wife had swatted him with one of the half dozen large pillows at the head of the bed.

"If you say your grandfather dragged you to a London brothel the way he did his two sons, I shall kick you from this bed and march you off the estate at gunpoint." She pushed away from him, sat up and swept the considerable length and weight of her hair behind her.

"My father and his brother are dead. How do you know—"

"Your mother. After your father's brother died, your mother refused to allow the duke near you. She did not want him to raise you the way he did his own sons. She...told me not long before she died." She looked away.

He had so many questions; not that her answers would change anything. His family was gone and Rhiannon was all he had left. His chest squeezed tight and a sort of achy pang, like the hurt of a sudden cold wind, lodged beneath his ribs. The truth. Right.

"It wasn't a brothel." Endymion lay on his back and stared at the tapestry-work canopy over her head. He combed his fingers through her tresses. "He set up a mistress for me in a house on Bruton Street when I was eighteen. After I came back from Oxford, I spent all of my time with my books or with Voil. The duke thought he and I were..."

His delicate bride, with the sheet and counterpane drawn across her naked breasts, snorted and rolled her eyes. "Even were he so disposed, Lord Voil would not put up with you as his paramour for five minutes."

"Undoubtedly. What of you, Rhee? Will you put up with me?"

"If I had taken a lover all these years? Would you put up with me?"

Rage roared through him. Primitive and so powerful, he clenched his fists to keep it inside where it belonged. She raised her chin, as bold and defiant as Boudica herself and more alluring than any woman he'd ever known.

"I'd be furious to the point of madness. Unfair of me, I know. But as you said, I am a bit of an *arse*."

"No, Your Grace, I said you were a complete horse's *arse*."

"Of course," he replied and forced his hands open. "So, you did."

She worried the side of her bottom lip, a gesture he remembered from childhood schemes and old hurts.

"I put her aside when my grandfather died," he confessed.

"You had the same mistress for seven years?"

"I was eighteen years old and an idiot, Rhee. She was my mistress the first year. After that, I did not share a bed with her. I only visited her when I needed to escape and find the peace and quiet of a household that would leave me alone."

"Escape?"

"The duke. Great Uncle Richard. Expectations." Endymion shook his head. "The silence in the house when I disappointed them or asked about the past." She didn't need to hear this. Those years were over and their treatment of him had only made him stronger.

"Why?"

"Why what?"

"Why didn't you share her bed? Why did you put her aside when the duke died?"

"I was married. I realized that honor in my dealings with everyone else was nothing if I did not honor my vows to you. When Lord Richard found out, he declared it a result of my mother's Methodist inclinations." A sudden heat lashed across his cheeks. He was blushing. In all his thirty-two years, he never, ever remembered blushing.

"Lord Richard is a disgusting, indolent *arse*," she declared as she slid next to him and lay her head on his shoulder. Dear God, at the gentle warmth that suffused him.

"Obviously a family trait." He put his arm around her. "Am I forgiven?"

"Hmmm," she murmured, tapping her chin with her finger.

"What does that mean?

"I'm trying to decide. I should be furious and ban you from my bed forever."

Endymion lay perfectly still.

"But as this woman must have been an excellent teacher and saved me from another night like our wedding night..." She ran her finger around his nipple and then across it.

"Please don't say another word about our wedding night. I am not certain my manhood can survive it."

"Or your stomach, for that matter," she said with a sly grin.

He rolled her beneath him and laced the fingers of her hands with his. "Shall I show you what else I learned, Your Grace?" He fused his mouth to hers in a deep, invasive kiss that left them both shaking.

A shadow rippled across her features for a moment. Then she smiled. The sort of smile Helen must have gifted Paris with, the sort of smile to cause a man to start a war rather than give up a woman he cannot live without.

"I should like that very much, Your Grace. Very much, indeed."

∽

Endymion hated reading in a moving coach. He especially hated reading estate ledgers in a moving coach when there were so many more inventive ways to spend time traveling slowly along a mud-sodden road toward God only knew where.

"Are you paying attention, Dymi?" his exasperated wife inquired. His wife he'd much rather have straddling his lap with the skirts of her blue kerseymere gown hiked up around her hips.

"You have been keeping two sets of accounts for the last seven years and only recording part of the estate's income because you suspect either my uncle or the estate manager he hired of embezzling said profits from the estate."

He wanted to believe her. He wanted to take her back to Pendeen and spend the rest of the evening in her bed. Babcock would get to the bottom of the discrepancies in the accounts. Rhiannon had admitted to underreporting the accounts, but where was the money? Two parts of his body—his brain and his cock—warred, a problem he'd never encountered before, and it irritated him.

She snatched the ledger from his lap and slammed it closed before dropping it into a leather portmanteau. "I don't *suspect*, I know. Apparently, that isn't good enough for you."

"My man of business will—"

"Ah, yes, Babcock, whom you trust, will go over my ledgers and solve all of my problems. Nothing for me to worry my silly female head over." She folded her arms across her chest and stared out the coach window into the late afternoon gloom.

"Would you like to tell me what this is truly about, Rhee? You've been nervous and petulant since you kicked me out of your bed and demanded I meet you in front of the house in a few hours dressed for travel. Where are we going? And more important, why?" He left unasked the question he most wanted answered.

Where was the woman he'd made love to most of the night? Where was the woman who'd fallen asleep in his arms and given him his first night's rest in as long as he could remember? He'd awoken to find her standing in the middle of her bedchamber, wrapped in that tatty, flannel robe, a scrap of parchment in her hand. She'd given him his orders and disappeared into her sitting room to summon her maid.

"Here," she said without turning away from the window, that same piece of paper in her outstretched hand. "I received this message last night. We are on our way to Zennor."

"Zennor?" His entire body went cold. Zennor, the tiny village he, his mother, and brothers had fled to after his father died, and the duke had them thrown from the house. His mother had gone by the name of Lizzie Bryant, and he and his brothers had used their ordinary middle names rather than the romantic names their father had given them.

Endymion understood better now his mother's reasons for trying to keep them hidden. She'd chosen an obscure village close enough, the duke might never suspect. Hiding in plain sight. He remembered now, the rumors had them living in Manchester, with her working as housekeeper rather than a tavern maid in an ancient, rundown inn. He honed his attention onto the message his wife had received.

The farmer, Wilson, is responsible for the accident at the mines.
He is to meet his master at The Mermaid's Tale.
Tomorrow evening as the sun sets.
I'll be watching.

The Mermaid's Tale, where his mother had worked. Where she had died, or so he'd been told.

"She was killed by a customer at the damned tavern she dragged you and your brothers to after your father died. What sort of end did she expect, subjecting all of you to such a disreputable, dangerous place?"

Lord Richard de Waryn was not known for his sympathetic nature. He'd been hard on Endymion to break him of his *lowborn ways*. He'd warmed to him as the years went by and these days, like many older gentlemen, he tended to keep to himself.

"Who sent you this message?"

"You are not the only one with spies in my household, Your Grace."

"My staff are not spies."

"And Lord Voil? What is he?"

"A malingering houseguest and a poor excuse for a spy." Endymion shoved his hands into the pockets of his dark blue hunting jacket. A storm brewed a few miles away. The chill he'd sensed earlier settled into his bones. The scents and scenery passing outside the lumbering coach, increasingly familiar, threatened to suffocate him. He tapped his forefinger against the top of his thigh. "Why could Voil not do this, or your Mr. Thomas?" He sounded bored and put out, just as he planned. He'd determined not to show even an inkling of the shroud of dread wrapping itself tighter and tighter around him.

"Josiah is a stranger in Zennor. He came with Papa from Yorkshire when they were both young men. Lord Voil would stick out like a whore in church." She turned away from the window, her brown eyes huge in a face pale beyond reason. "They look after their own in Zennor, Dymi. You are your mother's son, and it is time."

"Time for what?" Endymion spread his arms across the back of the seat. Even lacking the ducal crest, the unmarked coach afforded every comfort—wide, tufted, leather-covered seats, with thick carpeting on the floor and ornate carriage lamps on either side of the interior.

He adopted the pose of idle aristocrat, luxuriating in his riches, when his heart thudded like a blacksmith's hammer and his mind screamed at him to turn around and go home, to Pendeen, or better, to London. Seemed a practical idea until his gaze fell on her hands plucking at her skirts. And then his focus was drawn to her face and he knew. Against everything he'd ever learned at his grandfather's side, against all sense and logic, Endymion resolved to face whatever demons he must to keep her safe.

The coach slowed and pulled to a stop within the narrow confines of a ramshackle stableyard. The inn outside the coach window appeared equally weathered by time's unkind hand. Three stories tall, white-washed, with a pitched gabled roof, crooked windows, and a series of chimneys belching smoke into the waning light.

And hanging from a creaking, rusty arm, the faded sign he'd

seen in his nightmares for as long as he could remember. He stepped down the coach steps and studied the worn wood swinging above the tavern door. Thunder rumbled out to sea. The figure on the sign held him transfixed. The narrow lane behind him, the stableyard, everything fell away. Every hair on the back of his neck stood on end.

"Dymi?" A small hand, frail as fine china and strong as iron, slipped into his. "We need to go inside before we are seen. Can you... Do you think you..."

He grasped her hand, tightly, forcing himself not to crush it. "According to you and Voil, I spend too much time thinking and planning." He turned his back on the sign and still felt its eyes on him. "Is it too much to hope this tavern serves a decent pasty?"

"You'll be lucky if it serves a decent swill," the coachman muttered. He flipped the collar of his coat up around his neck.

"As we discussed, John," Endymion said as he led Rhiannon up the steps to the ancient oak door. He glanced down the road in the opposite direction from which they'd come. A chill shot through him. The road was empty, but he heard horses, horses galloping toward the inn, and then the blast of a musket so real he flinched.

"This is a bad idea," Rhiannon suddenly said. "John, take us back to *Gorffwys Ddraig*." She began to tug Endymion toward the coach.

Endymion shook his head against the fog of remembrance. "Bad ideas never stopped us as children, Rhee. Look sharp, John."

"Aye, Your Grace." The coachman strolled to the corner of the inn and settled onto the stone mounting block there, his legs outstretched and his hat pulled down over his eyes.

Rhiannon released his hand and pulled the hood of her long, black cloak over her head. Endymion quirked an eyebrow.

"Robert Wilson does not know you. He does, however, know me," she said and tucked her arm through his.

"Which is why you neglected to give me the particulars of this adventure until it was too late to lock you in the cellar," he muttered in her ear as they made their way through the crowded taproom toward a table in the back corner.

She snorted. "It might have worked had you not showed me every way out of that cellar when we were children."

"Short-sighted of me. Almost as short-sighted as bringing my wife to confront the man whose manhood she threatened to shoot off." He motioned her into the chair next to the wall. One by one, Endymion scanned the faces of the room's occupants and then dropped into the chair between his wife and the taproom. "Is he here?"

"Not yet. What did you discuss with my coachman?"

"I ordered him to watch for trouble, warn us if trouble arrives, and to drive the coach around to the back of the inn to meet us." He signaled the young tavern maid who wound her way through the maze of tables toward them.

"I don't suppose he told you he'd already had those exact instructions from me?" she asked, peering at him from beneath her hood like some mischievous fey creature.

"No, he did not." He didn't know which irked him more—his wife's cheek or her coachman's. *Her* coachman. Would he ever win over Rhiannon? For if he did not, the estate at Pendeen would never truly be his.

She covered his hand with hers. "They have answered to me for seventeen years, Dymi."

"And they allow you to run about Cornwall willy nilly with no thought to your safety?"

"It is not their place to allow or disallow me. They have kept me safe these seventeen years."

"When they can find you. How are they to see to your welfare when they don't know where you are half the time?" He clenched his fist under the table and cursed himself for a fool. Every word gave her the opportunity to hurt him.

"What can I do for you, guv'?" the maid asked when she finally reached their table.

"Two of your finest ales, if you please." Endymion flipped a gold crown onto the maid's tray. When she did not move, he glanced up to find her staring at him.

"You are—" The maid shut her mouth with a sharp click of her teeth. Endymion glanced down to find Rhiannon had leaned across him to wrap her hand around the young woman's wrist.

"Hello, Hannah," his wife said softly. "We need your silence, if it isn't too much trouble."

"Is he who I think he is?" the tavern maid asked.

"He is, and he is not here."

Endymion had never heard such a cryptic conversation in his life. A cold breeze swept in from the front of the tavern as a group of men pushed their way into the taproom.

The young woman, with hair black as night and eyes as blue as a summer sky, moved to block Endymion's view of the door. "Then you'd best take him up the stairs and down the back because the men who just came in have come in here every night for seventeen years."

Endymion erupted from his chair. Rhiannon grabbed his arm and pulled him toward the rickety stairs behind them. He turned on her, rage savaging every inch of his being.

"Not tonight, Dymi," she insisted. "Not like this."

"Go," the maid, Hannah, urged. "They have not seen you yet. Go."

He stood in the shadows and studied the faces of the four men dressed in ratty, old militia jackets. He did not recognize them, but something about them stoked a fire in him he suspected had burned for a very long time.

"We were meant to wait and see who meets Robert Wilson," Endymion said even as he allowed Rhiannon to pull him away.

"He's here all the time these past weeks," Hannah said as she took a quick peek over her shoulder. "I'll send word to Tall William. Go!"

Silent as a wraith, his wife led him up one flight of stairs and then another. As she started down the sloped floor of the second-floor corridor, Endymion stopped in his tracks. A narrow staircase rose to the third floor. The steps and bannister, hand-hewn and unfinished, pricked at his memory. He'd been here before, so much so he did not doubt he could close his eyes and ascend those steps as surely as he might those in his London townhouse.

Rhiannon came to him. She took his hand and tried to lead him away. Her face, white and strained, sent icy flares of warning through his body. And still he followed the lure of familiarity, no matter how laced with horror it seemed. He did not release her hand and she had no course but to follow him. At the top of those stairs, a narrow walkway led to what appeared to be another staircase leading down to the back of the inn. He had to bow his head to tread the walkway. To his left, Endymion saw exactly what he expected—a single door that led to the single room beneath the low-beamed ceiling.

"Dymi, don't," Rhiannon pleaded even as she peered behind them as if in anticipation of footsteps following. "You don't want to do this."

He heard her, she sounded far away, but he heard her. He raised the door latch and stepped into the chamber, Rhiannon's hand still clutched tightly in his. The lingering stench of damp and disuse permeated the room. He released her hand, strode to the window and threw open the shutters, flooding the room with the light of the rising moon. In spite of the disuse, the floors and walls, the corners and furnishings sported very little dust and no cobwebs. To the right stood an old four-poster bed, the mattress sagging beneath a holland cover. To the left, three cots stacked one atop the other rested against a bare white-washed wall.

There'd been other furnishings—a threadbare rug, a rocking chair, a table and stools. All gone, save in his memory. He let go of Rhiannon's hand and paced the confines of the room, in search of what he knew not. His breath, perhaps. He'd lost the ability to draw air into his lungs. Warmth? Bone-numbing cold washed over him in pounding waves.

"This is where she brought us," he said, each word pulled from the dark place where his previous life had been placed for safekeeping. "After my father died."

"Yes," Rhiannon replied from just inside the door.

"And this is where she died." Even as he said it, Endymion saw only darkness in his mind. Why could he not remember?

"Yes."

He turned back to the window, pushed it open and leaned out into the night.

Rhiannon drew in a breath behind him, half gasp and half something more visceral. The window offered a view of the ribbon of road leading away from the inn, over the hill, and across the moors to the sea. The road blazed across his mind. He'd ridden it on horseback a thousand times. And then one night...

The storm he'd heard in the distance moved closer. Lightning split the sky. The ensuing thunder cracked like gunfire. He started. Again, it sounded. And again. A musket. Not thunder, a musket. One shot, fired into the night. A warning. He and his brothers had incurred the wrath of the magistrate and the militia. The soldiers had lain in wait, but the musket shot had warned Endymion and his brothers, and they'd ridden away. They'd ridden away as their mother lay dying in this very room.

Endymion breathed deeply. He braced his hands against the window frame. His lungs burned. His head pulsed with the echoes of that single musket shot over and over again. His heart raced in time to the rumble of hoofbeats on the road. Above it all, the death wail of a woman lanced through him. The wail of a ghost, the ghost of The Mermaid's Tale, the ghost that had kept him from ever returning to Cornwall.

He dug his fingers into the wood of the window frame. *No!* He was the Duke of Pendeen. He was the master of his emotions, in control of every aspect of his life. Nothing and no one had the power to break him.

"Dymi." Her arms crept around him. The warmth of her body pressed his back. She clasped her hands over his heart. He covered her hands with his as she rocked him ever so slightly back and forth. "I don't know why I brought you here."

"I needed to remember," he rasped. "They murdered her because of us."

"No, Dymi, it was not your fault. It was never your fault."

"We rode as highwaymen—Hector, Achilles, and I—robbing my grandfather's friends. The militia came after us, but they murdered her. They murdered her because of us." The words came out in painful gasps. His throat tightened. His eyes burned.

"No." She slipped around him and held his face between her hands. "She would never want you to believe that. Your mother loved you. More than you will ever know."

"Why didn't I remember? My mother was murdered, and I didn't remember." He rested his forehead against hers. It helped. God forgive him, but it helped to lean against the slight woman Fate had joined him to all those years ago.

"You did remember, Dymi," she said and leaned up to kiss him. "Somewhere inside, you knew. They didn't want you to remember—your grandfather, your uncle. But I was here. I always remembered. I remember it all. I kept it for you until you were ready." He hugged her to him. Her tears dampened his waistcoat and shirt.

He tilted her face up and wiped her tears with his thumbs. "What a ramshackle husband you are saddled with, Your Grace. Broken into pieces, one foot in London and one foot in the past." He gazed into her eyes, anchored himself there. "You were mine to protect, Rhiannon, and I have done a bad job of it in every way."

"And you were always mine, Endymion. No matter how broken, you were always mine to pick up and put back together. Whatever has passed between us, I have not forgotten that." She rested her palm against his cheek.

He drew in a deep breath and then another. "Those men had something to do with it, Rhee. I cannot let it pass." He started around her. She wrapped both hands around his forearm.

"Not tonight. Your mother was born in this village, but most people do not remember you. You start something tonight and they will kill you. No one in Zennor will say a word about it."

"I am the Duke of Pendeen and those men murdered my mother," he snapped.

She rolled her eyes and grabbed his hand. They crept out onto the walkway. "The men in that taproom care not one whit who you are, Dymi. Their ancestors ate their own dead, for God's sake. They'll kill you and toss you into the sea without a second thought. This way." She picked her way carefully down the back staircase.

"Bloodthirsty lot," he muttered. "They'll kill me, but what of you?"

"We'll never know. If they take you, I have every intention of using the commotion to make my escape." They reached and slipped out the inn's back door. "There you are, John," she greeted the coachman. "To *Gorffwys Ddraig,* if you please. As quickly as you can."

Endymion had no sooner tossed her into the coach and

hefted himself in beside her than the conveyance rolled slowly from behind the tavern and turned quietly onto the road. Once they'd lost sight of the tavern, John sprung the horses and they raced toward home.

Home.

Endymion had not called any part of Cornwall home in a very long time. The raw remembrances he'd just experienced did not bode well for it ever being where he wanted to remain. He'd lost so much to this place. Yet, seated next to him, his hand clasped between hers, his wife had never lived anywhere else. She'd kept his family's estate, his grandfather's legacy, and Endymion's lost memories all these years. How much of the turmoil roiling inside him was the shadow of his mother's death and how much was the thought of returning to London and leaving Rhiannon here?

"Rhiannon, I—"

The coach jolted, slid and tilted. Endymion wrapped himself around Rhiannon as they slammed into the padded side. Two shots sounded over the frightened neighs of the horses. The coach stopped dead in the road.

Rhiannon, eyes wide, pushed out of his embrace and reached for the door handle.

"Stay here," Endymion ordered as he pushed her away from the door. He snatched a pistol from beneath the seat across from them and flung the door open.

"Look out, Your Grace," John shouted from the driver's bench where a man held a pistol to his head. The man, one of the ragged militia men from the inn, cuffed the coachman with the butt of his pistol.

Two more of the men approached Endymion from the front and rear of the coach.

"Drop the pistol, Your Grace," the man next to John ordered. "Don't make my friends take it from you."

Endymion heard a hammer being pulled back behind him.

Thank God, his wife never listened to him. He turned toward the man on the coach, aimed, and shot him between the eyes. Rhiannon leaned out of the coach and shot the man who approached from the rear. In the confusion, Endymion rushed the man who approached from the front, but failed to reach him before the man got a shot off. Once he knocked the man off his feet, Endymion pounded him senseless in a few punches.

"Your Grace!" John cried.

Endymion turned to find Rhiannon sprawled in the road. He stumbled to her side and rolled her over into his arms. He ran his hands over her and when he reached her face he encountered a wetness that appeared black when he held his hand up in the moonlight.

Blood.

"Rhiannon," he barked as he shook her. "Rhee, wake up." A living, breathing monster of fear clawed at the edges of his control. For her, he had to remain calm, when all he wanted to do was roar against the death and treachery that threatened to take the last, the only, the most treasured thing left to him in Cornwall.

The coachman thrust a handkerchief at him.

"Hand her to me," a voice spoke out of the darkness. A tall, rangy horse stepped onto the road as if from nowhere. The rider, dressed in black, wearing a tri-cornered hat with a white plume, reached a hand down to Endymion.

The clatter of hoofbeats coming from the direction of Zennor sounded in the distance.

"I suggest you and your coachman unhitch the horses and we all ride for *Gorffwys Ddraig* before the rest of those hired ruffians catch us." The man urged his horse forward until horse and rider entered the bright light of the full moon.

Endymion wiped blood from Rhiannon's face. He glanced up at the man leaning down from his horse, hand outstretched.

He shook his head, checked his wife's even breathing, and stared up at the man once more.

It...could not be.

"Achilles?"

"Hello, Dymi. Now hand your wife up here, and let's ride, shall we?"

CHAPTER 13

She'd fallen out of the horse chestnut tree. Again. Rhiannon's head throbbed like the very devil. This time she'd fallen on the front of her head rather than the back. She reached up to find a small pad tied to her forehead by a strip of linen around her entire head. She managed to open one eye and immediately closed it against the glare of her bedchamber suffused in light. Voices, male voices, rumbled a few feet away.

Papa?

No, these were young men. In her bedchamber. Eyes still clenched tightly shut, she ran her hands over the counterpane. It was rich and thick and not at all like the one on her bed at home. And there were entirely too many pillows on this bed. A scent caught her attention. She pulled one of the larger pillows to her face and inhaled.

Endymion.

She wasn't a little girl in the country home her father had bought from an impoverished lord. She was the Duchess of Pendeen in the duchess's bedchamber. In the duchess's bed, which she'd shared with Endymion against her every sensible instinct. Then they'd driven to…

Zennor.

The Mermaid's Tale and the room where Eliza Bryant de Waryn had died.

Men with guns.

"I don't understand any of this. Least of all, how my wife may be the only person who knows what happened that night. You let me believe you were dead for seventeen years, and she knew." Endymion was pacing and ranting. Even with her eyes closed she recognized his infuriated footsteps. "How am I to have any hope of sorting this out if you won't tell me?"

"She has only known these last ten years. As for the rest... what happened that night is not my story to tell."

Achilles.

Rhiannon did not know how or why Endymion's brother came to be at *Gorffwys Ddraig*, but she knew what it meant. It was time. Time to destroy the burgeoning bond between her and her distrustful husband. Time to end any hope of a real marriage with the boy she'd married, the man she now loved even more than she ever thought possible.

"Dammit, I am tired of the secrets, and the lies, and every man in Cornwall attempting to kill my wife," Endymion roared. "I need to know the truth."

"You need to stop swearing at your brother," Rhiannon said as she opened her eyes and gingerly, in broken stages, pushed herself into a sitting position on the pillows mounded against the headboard. Her head pounded with every beat of her heart and it took a moment for her blurred vision to clear. "And not every man in Cornwall is trying to kill me. Yet."

Achilles chuckled and touched two fingers to his head in silent salute.

Endymion took a step toward the bed and then stopped. He clasped his hands behind his back and pinned her with a stoic, unreadable gaze. "You should have stayed in the coach. You are fortunate the shot only grazed you. Dr. Douglas has ordered you to remain in bed for at least a week."

"No wonder she wouldn't come to you in London," Achilles said as he settled onto the arm of one of the fireside chairs. "Does he always sound so much like our father's *arse* of a father?"

"Not always," Rhiannon replied. Her entire life might be about to crumble around her, but Endymion had his brother back. She'd try to hold on to that much, at least.

"Leave us," Endymion ordered. "I want to speak with my wife."

"You want to browbeat her into answering all of your questions whether she knows the truth or not. You had ten years to ask our grandfather those questions. Why didn't you?"

"He can stay, Dymi. Let him stay, and I will tell you what you want to know."

"Very well." Endymion stood, unbending, as if questioning a disobedient servant.

"Sit down," she said, her voice weary and thin to her own ears. "My head hurts and I will not do this with you looming over me, forcing me to crane my neck. Your grandfather tried it with me the night you and I were married. It didn't work then either."

His mouth quirked the tiniest bit. He dragged the chair opposite his brother to her bedside and subsided into it, his arms braced on the chair's arms in what looked to be a completely uncomfortable pose. "Achilles says you were at the ruins the night we were captured. I thought I remembered your voice, but I wasn't certain. Why didn't you tell me that when we—"

"When we visited the ruins last week?" She took a deep breath, like a swimmer about to dive into an icy lake. "I did not want you to know I was there that night. I did not want you to know I was the one who led the duke's men to you."

"You what?" his words came out on a harsh whisper. He glanced back at his brother, who merely shrugged. "You hid us, and then you betrayed us?"

"I did."

"Why?"

"The duke promised you would not be harmed. I came to *Gorffwys Ddraig* to find out the truth of his intentions. Men were scouring the county for you. The militia had killed your mother, and some of them were involved in the search. I came here that night, and I heard some men talking. They'd sent the militia to kill all of you, your mother and brothers and you. With your mother dead, they planned to find you and kill you. The duke wanted you alive." It hurt so much to watch his face as confusion, disbelief, and betrayal chased across his features.

"I thought my brothers were dead. You betrayed us and put us through that nightmare to keep me safe?"

"Not entirely," she said and clutched handfuls of the counterpane in her fists.

"Rhiannon," Achilles warned. She looked at her husband's brother, smiled bitterly, and shook her head.

"He needs to know it all," she said, her voice shaking. "I did it to secure your hand in marriage. My father did not trust the duke to keep his word even with the dowry he offered him. Papa did not broach the subject with your grandfather until he had more incentives to offer His Grace than my dowry. Your location, your safe return, was one of them."

She'd been shot. She'd fallen from trees in her youth, from her horse only a few months ago. Had a calciner nearly bury her. The pain of those injuries paled next to the pain in her breast as she revealed the desperation of the girl she'd been to have him for her own. A stupid, foolish girl manipulated by her father and a monster who'd used her to capture the grandson he wanted only because he had no one else left.

"It is nice to know my hand was worth more than mere

money," Endymion snapped and pushed himself out of the chair. "You were willing to sacrifice my brothers' lives to become a duchess. No wonder my grandfather agreed to the marriage. I am certain he believed a woman like you would breed him ruthless grandsons to carry on the family name."

"She didn't sacrifice our lives, Dymi," Achilles said as he, too, rose from his chair. "She is the reason we escaped. She led the duke's men into the dungeon whilst we hid in the priest's hole."

"It doesn't matter, Achilles," Rhiannon said wearily. Endymion's face, his posture—stiff with anger and hurt—told her so. Nothing mattered now.

"She sent the tavern master from Zennor with horses, money, and food the next morning. We escaped."

"Where is Hector?" Endymion demanded.

"I don't know. Once we reached Portsmouth, we separated in case we were followed. I went to sea. He went to London. He may well be dead, but if he is, it is not Rhiannon's fault."

"He was ten years old."

"And had been riding the roads of the county robbing the coaches of the wealthy with us for over a year. He was a better shot and a bolder rider than either of us," Achilles's voice never rose above his normal, quiet tone.

They were quarreling, and she had no right to interfere. Dammit.

"You put him in danger," Achilles said. "I put him in danger. Rhiannon did the best she could to look out for him. If he is dead, whose fault is it, Dymi?"

"Enough," Rhiannon cried and held her head.

Endymion stepped to the bed and sat on the edge of the mattress. He pushed her hands away and lifted the bandage enough to check her wound. "You should rest," he said. He seemed almost embarrassed by his concern.

"I have hired a series of Runners since Achilles's return,"

Rhiannon said. She stared at Endymion's hand resting on the counterpane next to hers. "In ten years, they have found no sign of Hector in London, but they will continue to search so long as I pay them."

"You hired Runners in London, but did not pen a single word to let me know my brother was alive." Endymion stood and began to pace the room again.

"Had I done so, would you have even known, Your Grace? How many people read your correspondence before you deign to waste your time with it? I wrote letters in the beginning. They were answered by your uncle or not at all."

"It wasn't her fault," Achilles interrupted. "I made her swear not to tell you."

"For God's sake, why?"

A sharp, distinct knock at the door produced a sudden silence. Achilles pulled a pistol from the waist of his black breeches. Endymion went to the nightstand and retrieved the pistol Rhiannon kept there. When she raised an inquiring eyebrow, he shrugged and placed himself between her and the door.

"Oh, for pity's sake," she muttered. "Come in, Bea."

The maid opened the door just enough to slip inside, a torn, wrinkled piece of parchment in her hand. She gave both men a curious look and curtsied. "Your Graces. My lord."

Achilles shook his head.

Bea crossed the carpets to Rhiannon's bedside. Endymion stepped aside when it appeared the woman intended to walk over him. She handed Rhiannon the parchment. "Tall William had this from his cousin. A boy brought it to the kitchens door."

"What is it?" Endymion demanded.

"A message for Her Grace," Bea replied curtly.

Achilles laughed, which drew a fulminating glare from his brother.

Rhiannon hid a painful smile. They could afford to tease Endymion. She could not. He was withdrawing from her, the rending tear of it as painful as any wound. Every word, every gesture, drew him farther away from her and back into the role he'd played all these years. She turned her attention to the message.

Robert Wilson met two men after you left.
One was a well-dressed gentleman I do not know.
The other was Captain Randolph.

She handed the note to her husband, who read it and handed it to his brother.

"Is that why you came back?" Endymion asked Achilles. "Did you suspect he was—"

"Involved in our mother's murder?" Achilles replied with a shrug. "I did. I hoped he would lead us to the other two, but he is far more sly than I ever credited."

"You suspected him, and you allowed him to—"

"I did," Rhiannon declared. "I was not convinced he was responsible for the accidents, but I suspected him of plundering the estate's coffers. I decided it was wise to keep my enemy close."

"Of course, you did." Endymion scrubbed his hands over his face. "Is he one of the men you heard that night, Rhee?"

"I don't know," she replied. "I thought I'd never forget those voices, but there was the storm, and when I heard them, all I thought to do was run to Papa. I became lost. Your grandfather never allowed lamps in the corridors at night. When I finally found Papa, he persuaded me to—"

"Betray me and help deliver me to the parson's noose like the fatted calf. I remember that part." He walked across the room to the fireplace and turned to face her, his expression austere to the point of coldness.

"You made a bad bargain of it, Rhee," Achilles offered. "Pity it is too late to renege on the deal."

"None of this is amusing," Endymion snapped. "This is my life you are toying with, dammit."

"What life, Dymi?" his brother asked. "She may have delivered you into the duke's hands, but you stayed there quite comfortably these seventeen years. You've been living the life he told you to live. When will you start living for yourself?"

"You have been riding the roads as a highwayman and hiding your existence from me, from your own brother. Whose life are you living?"

"I hid my existence from you because I did not trust you, Dymi. From all accounts, you have become our grandfather's creature. And our grandfather may well have been behind all of this—our mother's murder, the attempt to kill us, the attempts on Rhiannon's life." Achilles folded his arms in a typical give-no-quarter pose too similar to his brother to be denied.

"Our grandfather is dead."

"And has a long damned reach, even from the grave," Achilles affirmed. "He continues to dictate your actions."

"Now you sound like my wife," Endymion replied, each word laced with icy disdain. "Neither of you knew him the way I did. He—"

"He threw us from the house the day our father died," Achilles shouted. "It is his fault our mother was forced to work as a tavern maid. It was his fault we were forced to take to robbery to feed ourselves. It is his fault the militia came after us. The militia led by Captain Randolph. The militia that killed our mother. How can I trust you when I never, ever trusted him?"

Silence settled over the room like a shroud.

Beatrice crept quietly to the door into Rhiannon's dressing room. Rhiannon wished she might join her there. It was bad enough Endymion despised her. What would he have left if he and Achilles broke with each other just as they were reunited?

The two men stared at each other—Achilles arrogant and defiant, Endymion cold and austere, as she had made him with her confession.

"There is nothing we can do about the past," Endymion finally said. "If the message from Zennor is true, a man in one of this estate's most trusted positions has plotted with others to murder my duchess. I am going to set safeguards in place here at *Gorffwys Ddraig,* and then Lord Voil and I will go in search of Robert Wilson and his master. Will you ride with me?" he asked his brother.

"Always," Achilles replied.

Endymion turned to Rhiannon, his hands once more clasped tightly behind his back. He appeared more reserved and distant than the day he'd arrived in Cornwall. Had it been less than three weeks ago?

"You will do me the favor of keeping to your chambers until this man is found. I cannot afford to risk the lives of the household running after you."

"As you wish, Your Grace. Are you certain you would not prefer to lock me in the cellar?" She had lied to him, true, but she'd not live the rest of her life as the duke's cowed and subservient wife. She'd worked too hard to become a woman worthy of the title her father had bought for her.

"I would if I thought it might hold you. We will discuss this day's revelations further once this business of your safety is done." He gave her one of the constrained bows she so despised and marched to the door.

"To what end, Your Grace? I am already tried and convicted. What is left to discuss?"

He hesitated, his hand flat against the door. Then he squared his shoulders and left.

Rhiannon collapsed against the pillows. Tears, unshed over

years of loneliness and shame, clogged the back of her throat. Her eyes burned as if forced open against a salty wind. "You must stay, Achilles. You must stay with him. He will never forgive me, and he will need you."

Her highwayman brother-in-law strolled to her bedside, sat down, and took her hand. "He came back for you, Rhee. Against all the ghosts and pain and guilt, he came back for you."

"He came back for an heir, an heir to your damned grandfather's title. Nothing more."

"Tell yourself that if it helps. I can tell you from experience, lying to yourself may help for a while, but it will not help forever." He kissed her hand, rose, and walked to where Beatrice held his plumed hat in her hand. "You will look after her, Miss Smith?"

"Of course, sir." Beatrice curtsied, then handed him his hat. Her eyes followed him as he crossed the room and went out the door.

"The duke isn't the only de Waryn brother who is criminal handsome, is he, my friend?" Amidst the rubble of her breaking heart, Rhiannon held hope her wounded friend and her rogue of a brother-in-law might become more than friends.

"Don't be ridiculous," Beatrice replied, her face still flushed. "You told him. His Grace, I mean. He knows it all now."

"Not quite all," Rhiannon said.

"No," Beatrice agreed. "Not quite all. What do you intend to do?"

"I don't think he will ever forgive me, Bea. What can I do?"

CHAPTER 14

Endymion swung into the saddle and turned his horse back the way they'd come. He'd spent last night securing every inch of *Gorffwys Ddraig* against the one enemy he now knew and a hoard of others he suspected. Every male servant, those he'd brought from London and those in service at the house, had been armed and assigned posts. Even Babcock and poor Meeks, Endymion's valet, had been pressed into service. Between them, Endymion and his brother remembered every possible hidden door and coal chute, every window where one might pry a latch.

His brother.

Even now, he scarcely believed the taciturn man riding next to him was Achilles, the brother he'd thought lost to him. The man Rhiannon had supposedly saved and then kept hidden for no reason Endymion understood. He didn't understand any of it, and he didn't understand the pulsing ache in his chest when his thoughts turned to his wife and all she'd done to betray him and prove his grandfather right.

"Do we have a plan or are we to simply follow you until you ride into the sea?" Voil's question stopped Endymion's mind from wandering to Rhiannon for the thousandth time since the marquess and Achilles had insisted on riding out with him just after dawn.

Endymion pulled up his horse and surveyed the fields on one side of the lane and the forests on the other. He looked back to the rather fine manor house their quarry called home. The man's servants had balked at admitting them until they realized the Duke of Pendeen was at the door. He, Voil, and Achilles had made quick work of searching the house in spite of the servants' assurances Captain Randolph was not at home.

"If he hired the men who overtook our coach, he will know by now something has gone wrong," Endymion said. "If the fact we survived has reached him—"

"If?" Voil fought to control his horse as it danced nervously in the middle of the road. "The only servants who gossip worse than those in London are those who work in a country house. There is nothing else to occupy their time."

"Not this country house," Achilles replied, the most he'd spoken since Endymion had introduced him to Voil. "The duchess's household is loyal to her to the death. They keep her secrets as their own. No word of last night's events came from *Gorffwys Ddraig*."

"How can you be so certain?" Voil asked.

"I have been back in Cornwall and in communication with Her Grace these ten years, when all of England believes me dead."

"I take your point," Voil agreed.

Endymion swallowed against the bitterness and rage roiling in his veins. "I have no doubt the household—hell, the entire estate—is more than capable of keeping secrets. They have taken their instruction from their mistress."

Voil and Achilles exchanged a look and turned their horses toward *Gorffwys Ddraig*.

"Where are you going?" Endymion asked as he urged his horse after them.

"To find some food and a warm bed for an hour or two," Voil replied. "This villain has gone to ground, Pendeen. I hunt neither fox nor partridge nor man without some food in my belly."

"He's right. We've been at this for hours," Achilles agreed, even as he divided his attention between the road ahead and the way behind, as alert as any fox upon hearing the first cries of the pack. "If he wasn't alerted before now, his servants will see to it."

"There are at least a dozen places between here and the house where he might be. I want to search—"

"Tall William has cousins in every village in the county," Achilles snapped. "If our man pokes his head into a tavern, inn, blacksmith's or bakehouse, we will know of it within the hour. You aren't looking for the man Wilson met at The Mermaid's Tale. You are looking for a way to avoid your wife."

"I still cannot believe you went to The Mermaid's Tale and left me behind," Voil groused as they walked their weary horses down the country lane marked on either side by towering gorse hedges. "If we did not encounter this villain, we might have at least caught sight of the famous ghost. I would dearly like to have seen her so I might—"

"Look at my brother," Endymion suggested, suddenly too tired to play the duke with his friend. "He looks very like her."

"She was our mother," Achilles replied to Voil's grim face and unasked question. "She was murdered in the room where we lived above The Mermaid's Tale and the man we seek was likely involved."

"Dear God," Voil murmured. "I did not know. Pendeen, I—"

"God was not there," Endymion said. "If he was, he did not heed three young boys when they heard the news and prayed it was not true."

"How is it you were spared?" Voil asked.

"We were—" Endymion started.

"We were riding the county as highwaymen, robbing our grandfather's wealthy friends and neighbors," Achilles said with a grin Endymion was seeing for the first time.

"Wait." Voil pulled his horse to a complete stop. "The Duke of Pendeen, the most upright, stiff-rumped, rigidly scheduled peer ever to take up a cause in Parliament, was a highwayman?"

"A good one, too," Achilles added.

Voil roared with laughter, which flushed a covey of birds from beneath the hedges.

"I will never hear the end of it now," Endymion complained as he struggled to keep his shying horse from rearing.

They urged their horses forward once more.

"You never told him any of this? Your closest friend?" Achilles asked as they passed through the gates at the head of the drive to *Gorffwys Ddraig*. "It seems your duchess isn't the only one who keeps secrets."

"She bartered our lives for a title, Achilles. She betrayed us and kept it from me for seventeen years. How can I ever trust her again?"

"Ask her," Achilles suggested.

"Ask her what?" The turrets come into view above the wall of yew trees across the front of the house. A strange quickening settled in Endymion's chest. He'd loved the house as a child. The joy of his childhood at Gorffwys Ddraig had ended the day his grandfather's brother had driven them out those doors into a world of poverty and shame. His grandfather had saved him from that poverty. The late duke had given Endymion a life he'd often dreamed of in the nursery of this very place. Rhiannon loved this place as he had all those years ago. She'd kept it for him, treasured it when he could not. Why?

"Why," Achilles said as they stopped at the top of the hill.

"Ask her why she did what she did, why she has kept all of these secrets for a family never really her own."

"She did it to make herself a duchess. What other reason could there be?"

"I did not want you to know I was alive because I feared our grandfather had made you his creature," Achilles confessed. "Apparently, I was right."

"I don't understand," Endymion said, a queer sort of notion skulking in the back of his mind.

"You've been here three weeks," Achilles's exasperation fairly bled from his tone. "Have you spent any of that time actually talking to your wife?"

"He's been wooing her," Voil, monumentally unhelpful, offered. "He took her on a picnic."

"A picnic." Achilles shook his head. "One picnic? Did our grandfather geld you?"

"Wait until you read the letter he wrote ordering Her Grace to London in order to breed an heir. The first letter, might I add, he had written to her in seventeen years."

Voil and Achilles were enjoying this conversation entirely too much. But Achilles's question drew his mind from the dangerous man stalking Rhiannon, the indignation and hurt he felt at her betrayal, and everything else that had been crowding his thoughts since he'd walked into the room at the top of the stair in The Mermaid's Tale.

What would make a woman do the things she had done—the bad and the good?

"What the devil?" Voil snapped.

Voil and Achilles dismounted and ran toward a figure lying next to one of the rampant dragon statues that flanked the drive. Endymion slid from his horse and joined them at the fallen man's side.

"William," Endymion shouted as he shook the fallen man's shoulder. "Tall William. What happened?"

CHAPTER 14 169

The footman stirred, opened his eyes and winced as he lifted a hand to the back of his head. "Your Grace." He struggled to push up on his elbows. His eyes widened. "He's here, Your Grace. He knew about the tunnels. He's here."

As one, Endymion and Achilles looked to the far side of the statue where one of the stones that comprised its base had been removed to reveal a ladder.

"Stay with him, Voil," Endymion ordered as Achilles started down the ladder.

Rhiannon.

~

"When he ordered you to stay in bed, I never actually believed you'd obey," Bea said as she removed the uneaten tray of food from Rhiannon's bed.

"Isn't this what ladies do when nursing a broken heart? Lie in bed and go into decline?"

Bea snorted. "Ladies do who don't know the meaning of the word love and cannot exert themselves to thump some sense into the man they love. We don't breed women like that in Cornwall." She placed the tray outside the corridor door and gathered up the clothes she'd stripped off Rhiannon after Endymion had carried her into the bedchamber shouting for Bea to find a physician. Bea had related the tale with much rolling of eyes and hand gestures, but Rhiannon didn't make much of it. He had not known the truth then. He did now.

Bea gave her a look of mock disapproval and went into the dressing room to see to the clothes in her arms.

Rhiannon sighed, flung the covers back, and scooted to the edge of the bed. With a few sweeps of her feet, she found her slippers and shoved her feet into them. She shrugged into her robe and glanced back at the bed. She'd fallen asleep clutching Endymion's pillow in her arms. What a fool she'd been to think one night with him would be enough. The love she'd labeled a girlish crush had not died, nor had it failed. Instead, it had become something far worse. Living these weeks with him, watching him remember the agony and tragedy that had been his life, her love for him had grown. In spite of his grandfather, he'd become a good man—stiff, arrogant, confused, and somewhat broken, but a good man. The man she'd always known he would be. Her fourteen-year-old self had seen those qualities in him and had wanted that man for her own. Even if she had to gather the broken pieces of that man and put him together again.

She walked to the window and pushed aside the drapes. He'd left before dawn, or so she'd been told. How long would he persist before he gave up the hunt and returned to London? And when he left? Who would put the pieces of *her* broken heart together again? She had to decide how much of herself she was willing to risk to win Endymion's love. No tricks. No leverage. No Papa. No plotting old duke. All she had was her love for Dymi and her determination.

A latch clicked behind her. The accompanying creak of the opening door grated on her ears, made sensitive by her head wound. "Bea, remind me to tell Vaughn to have that door oiled. It's disgraceful."

"No more disgraceful than a filthy coal miner's daughter passing herself off as a duchess."

Rhiannon resisted an urge to grip the drapes. Her blood ran as ice in her veins, but she refused to cower or show fear.

"Captain Randolph," she said as she turned to face him. "What can I do for you this morning?"

"I think we both know why I am here, girl. They should have allowed me to end you long ago, but you served a purpose. Until now." Dressed in clothes far more expensive and finely tailored than any estate steward might afford, he prowled her bedchamber very like the rat she'd always considered him. She'd never liked him, but could not put into words her aversion to his presence on the estate.

"And who might they be, Captain? If I am to be murdered by a hired lackey, I'd like to know who pulls your strings." Rhiannon sidled away from the window toward her bedside table. She spied a panel along the far wall where an inset door she'd never seen before stood ajar.

"I'm no lackey, you jumped up bitch. I am the only person with the stomach to do what needs be done. Did you tell your husband how his mother died? Does he know what she did?"

"He doesn't know. Which begs the question, how do you know? Were you there, Captain, when the mother of the future Duke of Pendeen died?"

"I took a great deal of pleasure in ending that whore and two of her bastards. Pity I missed the oldest, but we'll get him eventually."

Whore...her bastards... She recognized that voice. After all these years, her enmity for the steward she'd been forced to accept became clear.

"Eliza de Waryn was no whore and her sons are no bastards. Who sent you, Captain?"

"All evidence of her marriage to the late duke's youngest son is missing. Your husband will be declared a bastard."

"Missing?" Rhiannon maneuvered herself around the bedside table. She allowed the sleeve of her robe to fall over her hand and thrust it behind her back to try and open the drawer. A candlestick teetered and thumped to the floor. The slightest of board creaks from beyond the heretofore unseen door threatened to draw the captain's attention. She stepped closer to him and kicked the fallen candlestick toward the far side of the room. "The evidence is not missing. It is safely tucked away where neither you nor your masters will ever find it."

The color leached from his florid face. "Where is it, you Yorkshire whore?"

"Ah! You *told* them it was gone, but you didn't know who took it, did you? Just as you told them His Grace's brothers were killed trying to escape and you had their bodies thrown into the sea. What will you tell *them* when they discover those boys survived?"

"Liar! Damn you!" He raised his pistol.

"Rhiannon! Down!" Endymion erupted from the hidden door and launched himself at Captain Randolph.

She dropped to her knees and pulled her pistol from behind her back. The captain's pistol went off, with the shot whizzing past her head to dig into the headboard. Endymion wrestled the pistol from him and tossed it aside. The captain caught Endymion beneath the chin with a powerful punch, rolled away, and pulled a second pistol from his waistband. He rose to his knees and aimed at Endymion. The blast and smoke of three pistols firing at once deafened and blinded her.

"Dymi," she cried. Dear God, not now. Not like this. She dropped her smoking pistol and crawled to his side. "Dymi, answer me. Are you hurt? Dymi!"

Flat on his back, he gripped her arms and shook her. "What were you doing, taunting him like that? He could have killed you. Do you have any sense at all?" He dragged her into his arms and buried his face in her hair.

"I don't know if she has any sense," Achilles drawled as he kicked the captain's dead body over, "but she is a better shot than either one of us. Right between the eyes, Your Grace. Nicely done. The throat, Miss Smith. Another handy shot."

Rhiannon and Endymion turned to see the white-faced lady's maid, smoking pistol in hand. "Your shot pierced his heart, Mr. de Waryn. I'd say we all had a hand in it."

"Indeed," Achilles replied as he crossed the room and pried the weapon from Beatrice's hand.

Endymion shoved to his feet and helped Rhiannon stand.

CHAPTER 14 173

The pound of running feet and clamor of shouts approached the bedchamber door. Turpin's sharp barks added to the din.

"He was one of them, Dymi." Rhiannon gripped the lapels of his coat. "His voice. I recognized his voice. After all these years, I knew. He was one of the men in the library plotting to kill your family. You were right, Achilles."

"Yet you did everything you could to infuriate him. Evidence of my parents' marriage? Really, Rhiannon?" Endymion was dirty, disheveled, sweaty, and very much alive. The pompous toad.

"We should announce all is well, Miss Smith," Achilles suggested, "before the entire household breaks in here, guns blazing."

"An excellent idea," Bea murmured as they slipped out Rhiannon's bedchamber door.

"Rhiannon, I cannot—"

She pressed her fingers to Endymion's lips. "May we have this argument in a room without a corpse bleeding all over my Aubusson?"

He glanced at the captain's body, grabbed her hand and dragged her through the dressing room into his bedchamber. Turpin, who had been let into the ducal bedchamber amid the chaos, cavorted about them, punctuating his joy with barks and swipes of his tongue.

"Your dog is no guard dog if he is only allowed to guard the kitchens, Your Grace," Rhiannon said in an attempt to calm the temper she saw rising in his eyes.

"What need have I for a guard dog when I have a wife who is determined to place herself in danger at every turn?" He strode to the Chippendale commode across the room and poured a brandy, which he downed in a single gulp.

"Dymi, I am not responsible for the danger that has followed us since the night your mother died. The men I heard that night are. Your grandfather is. Had he accepted your father's choice of bride, had he looked after all of you once your father died, none of this would have happened."

"Had you come to London when I sent for you, what happened last night and today would not have happened. You cannot continue to live your life in this fashion. Keeping a viper employed to discover who his employers might be. Going into the mines to test head lamps. Threatening to shoot a farmer instead of allowing the bailiff or magistrate to remove him. Your Mr. Thomas caught Wilson attempting to bribe some smugglers into taking him to Scotland. He confessed to causing the accident at the mines."

"Young Bob was right. I should have shot him when I had the chance."

Endymion grabbed her by the shoulders and pushed her toward the fireside chair.

"Dymi, stop it. What are you doing?" He was beginning to frighten her.

He ran his hands through his hair, walked away, then returned.

"I don't know how much of this my grandfather was responsible for, but he never lied to me or betrayed me. He raised me to be a man of sense and responsibility. The sort of man who would never put others in danger or risk my life to prove my independence."

"What independence, Dymi?" Her heart clenched, and her earlier determination to fight for his love crumbled. "He's been dead for seven years and you still aren't free."

"Free? I am bound to the dukedom, to its people, to my position, and to a wife I never chose, but for whom I am responsible. I will never be free."

The truth, at last. He saw her as a responsibility. An unwanted one, at that. He'd always see her as such. As much as she loved him, she refused to live with a man who thought so little of her.

"I can free you of at least part of that burden, Your Grace." She stood and pushed her way past him. "As the mystery of the threat against me is solved and I no longer have to worry about a thieving, murderous steward, I wish you and Lord Voil a safe journey to London. I will manage this part of the dukedom and free you to do whatever it is you find more important and less onerous. Don't give a thought to those of us who prefer to dwell in the unsophisticated, unscheduled wilds of Cornwall."

She reached the door and turned. He gripped her elbow and snatched her into his arms

His eyes wild and his voice hoarse, he demanded, "How much can a man lose before he has nothing left of himself?" He kissed her, a fierce taking of her mouth, her breath, and, she feared, her very soul. She answered him with a fierceness and passion of her own. Taking and taking the last of his love she would ever taste. It was too much. There were no more pieces of her heart to break. She pushed him away.

"There are many ways to lose, Dymi. Just as there are many ways to allow someone to take things away. I won't allow you to take anything else from me." She snatched the bandage from her head, dropped it on the floor and walked out of his chamber into the now-empty corridor, save for Bea and Achilles.

"Where shall we go, Your Grace?" Bea asked as she looped her arm through Rhiannon's.

"Somewhere a lady might take to her bed and go into decline for a day or two." Rhiannon blinked back the tears that refused to stay behind her aching eyes.

"The green bedchamber is made up," Bea suggested.

As they passed him, Achilles caught Rhiannon's hand and squeezed.

"He didn't come back for me, Achilles," Rhiannon told him as she allowed Bea to lead her away. "He came back to convince himself he was right to leave."

CHAPTER 15

She was avoiding him. Again. For two days, she'd taken her meals in the chamber she'd chosen after the death of Captain Randolph, and only left that chamber when she was assured he had left the house. Then she secreted herself in her study and tended to the business of the estate. Business he had Babcock check over every night.

Now, he had no choice but to confront her and present his plans for her in person. He descended the stairs to the entrance hall and spotted Voil and Achilles deep in conversation. They each handed a flustered Vaughn a small leather pouch that clinked in the butler's hands.

They were at it again. Betting on his inability to persuade his wife to—

"Your Grace," Vaughn announced as he slipped the pouches into his pocket, "Her Grace is in the rose garden awaiting you."

"Thank you, Vaughn. If either of you two follow me, I will order Cook to keep that basket of pasties she baked for our journey, Voil," Endymion said as he walked out the front door.

He reached the terraces and paused on the top of the stairs that led down several levels of blooming flower gardens, ending at the rose garden that rolled out to the edge of the ha-ha. Rhiannon sat on a bench amidst the rows upon rows of rose bushes. She sat very primly, gazing down the length of the garden with perfect posture, dressed in green with her hair done up in the latest style from London. She wore no bonnet, but her hands were covered in some sort of lacy gloves.

He'd lain awake most of the night. He'd had no choice. The memories, the secrets revealed, and the events of the past few days played through his thoughts over and over. He'd arrived at few conclusions. It appeared, over the last seventeen years, everyone had controlled his life save himself. Captain Randolph had taken his family. Rhiannon had taken his hand in marriage. His grandfather had taken his freedom and given him order, an education, and a way to survive, but at a cost he'd never imagined.

As if she sensed his presence, Rhiannon turned and gazed up at him. His heart slowed. He forced himself to stroll casually down the steps when every instinct begged him to run. To gather her in his arms and take her to a place where there were no dukedoms or secrets or pasts full of lies and ghosts. That world did not exist. But he wanted her in his world, even if he had no idea why, or how that could be achieved.

"I am here, Your Grace, as commanded," she said when he came to stand before her. "What are my orders?"

"I would not have to issue commands if you were not so intent on hiding from me."

"We have lived separately for seventeen years. We have lived in the same house for nearly a month. Who is hiding from whom?" She turned her attention to her hands.

"I am not hiding. I am, that is, Voil and I are... I have a great deal of business to conduct in Town. Rather, it is my intention to return to London this afternoon." What was it about her that turned him into a stammering idiot?

"I am aware, Your Grace. I wish you a safe—"

"I have decided you will accompany me." He clasped his hands behind his back and fixed his attention on a curl determined to fly free of her coiffure.

"I see," she replied, her voice uncharacteristically quiet and sweet. "For what purpose?"

"I am not convinced you are out of danger. I prefer to have you in London until I am certain the danger is past. I think the running of the estate has taken a great deal of your time and effort. You are the Duchess of Pendeen. You deserve an easier, less strenuous life. I will leave Babcock to put things in order here and to hire a qualified and fair steward to run the estate. You will—"

"No." She rose gracefully and started up the steps toward the house.

"I beg your pardon?" He knew it would not be easy, not where Rhiannon was concerned. He ran up the steps to catch her. "What do you mean, no?"

"The same thing I meant when I turned down your last invitation to London." She whirled and nearly knocked him down the steps. "How dare you try to take Pendeen away from me?" She poked his chest with a finger. "You may leave Babcock here, if you like. I am certain he will send you a detailed report of my every order, my every purchase, and every single entry on the estate ledgers."

He had no choice but to back down the steps as she continued to poke and rage at him. "That isn't—"

"I have lied to you, forced you to marry me, kept your brother's return from you, and I am certain I have not run this estate as you or your precious grandfather would prefer." Her eyes were bright with unshed tears. "I will live the rest of my life here alone, without husband or children, and that will be punishment enough for my crimes. I will not be carted away from the only people who care for me just so you can parade me through the ballrooms and drawing rooms of

London and remind me of all the wrong I have done to you. I won't."

"How is offering you a life of ease and privilege a punishment?" he shouted. She saw life with him as punishment? The force of this pain was far too powerful to be wounded pride.

"That isn't what you are offering me and you know it, Your Grace. You are dragging me off to control me the way your grandfather controlled you."

"I am weary as the devil of hearing about my grandfather's control. I am my own man, madam. And as Duke of Pendeen, your husband, and my own man, I *will* have my wife with me in London where I *choose* to live."

"Where *you* choose to live?" Her chest heaved against the confines of her muslin dress. Her bottom lip trembled and then stilled. "Leave me here, Dymi. I am useful here. I serve a purpose. I can do nothing for you in London."

"You can provide me an heir," he replied, even as his mind provided a thousand things she might do for him. A thousand things he needed from her and feared only she might provide. He could not make sense of any of it.

"So you can raise him the way you were raised?" She shook her head. "You are a good man, Endymion, but there is something broken in you, something lost. I don't want a child of mine to grow up believing duty is a cage and needing and trusting anyone is a weakness."

"Lest you forget, you may already carry my child." Was it weakness to hope he might have that to tie her to him?

"Mrs. Davis worked as a midwife. I asked her when I might take you to bed and not risk getting with child. There is little to no chance, Your Grace, when one schedules marital relations correctly."

He was stunned.

"Why?"

"Not all dangers are to the body, Dymi. Some dangers are to

the soul." She reached up to run her forefinger across his lips. "I can't do it. I can't go to London. I can't have a child with a man who gives me nothing of himself, least of all, his trust. We both did foolish things when we were children. I forgave you long ago. You will never forgive me. And that leaves us where we have always been. Apart." She shrugged. "Perhaps it is for the best."

She started back up the steps. He caught her hand.

"Why, Rhiannon?"

"I've told you."

"No, why? Why did you want to marry me? What made you do…all those things to make me your husband?"

"You don't know?"

"No, I don't." He searched the past for an answer, just as he'd done all night. Achilles said he'd know if he just thought about it, but Endymion truly did not understand. Perhaps she was right. Perhaps he was irreparably broken.

"It doesn't matter, Dymi. I shouldn't have done it. If could undo it, I would. I would grant you that freedom, at least."

"Rhee, I don't understand."

"Goodbye, Dymi."

He stood at the bottom of the steps surrounded by roses and watched her go. The clatter of carriages arriving under the portico made the decision for him. It was time he returned to London. When he reached the top of the steps, Voil and Achilles waited for him.

"I take it she said no," Voil said, not bothering to put his inquiry in the form of a question.

"Which of you betted she'd say yes?" Endymion walked past the carriages being loaded under Babcock's capable supervision.

"Neither," Achilles replied. "Our bet was on something entirely different."

"What might that be?"

"Why are we headed to the stables?" Voil asked.

"I am going for a ride. You may accompany me, if you wish."

The two of them looked at him as if he'd lost his wits. Just as well. He was beginning to think he had. He hoped a ride might help him to find them.

They rode the entire estate, from the cliff's edge that threatened to drop into the sea, to the rolling green fields dotted with sheep, to the mines, and through the forests. They rode through the village where men doffed their caps and bowed, and women curtsied. Children stared, as they had every right to do. They rode to the ruins where Voil and Achilles remained on their horses whilst Endymion climbed to the top of the tower and slowly circled the battlements, studying the land like a Latin text in search of an answer that eluded him.

He descended to the tower chamber where they'd hidden the night his mother died. The voices were silent now, save for one. He listened this time, truly listened, and the odd, murky scrap of an idea at the back of his mind grew clearer. Once he remounted his horse, he turned toward the village once again.

"You are certain you won't come to London with us, Achilles?" he asked after they'd ridden in silence for a while.

"There are two more men out there, Dymi. I intend to find them."

"And after that?" Voil asked.

"Cornwall is my home," Achilles said. "I'll not let anything or anyone keep me from it. London holds nothing for me. It never has."

"Why did she do it, Achilles? Why did she want to marry me?"

"The proper question is why does she still want to be married to you?" Voil suggested.

"She has no choice, Voil."

"Your wife does not strike me as the sort of woman who lets others make choices for her," Voil replied.

"Why do you want to be married to her, Dymi?" his brother asked.

"I've made a muddle of it."

"Why did she do it? Why did she do something she knew you'd hate her for? Why did she do any of it?" Achilles asked with a disgusted shake of his head. "She is married to you for the rest of her life. Uncle Richard has offered her a great deal of money to have the marriage annulled."

"He what?"

"Have I told you how much I despise your uncle, Pendeen?" Voil offered, as he had on numerous occasions.

"Why did she do it?" Achilles asked once more.

Endymion stopped his horse. He closed his eyes and filled his lungs with the bright summer Cornwall air. He remembered. He remembered her face the night they'd married. He remembered her face as he came down the stairs on his return to Cornwall. He remembered her face in the room at The Mermaid's Tale, her touch, and words of comfort. He drew each vision in like air, her face, always her face, and her voice, and her touch. And he knew. Why she married him. And why he needed her, like the very air he breathed in the gentle heat of a Cornwall summer.

"I need a favor," he shouted as he urged his horse into a gallop. "Of the both of you."

A favor, some luck, and a chance in hell it wasn't too late.

CHAPTER 16

The case clock at the end of the corridor struck three. Rhiannon lay in the comfortable bed in the green guest chamber and stared at the ceiling where shadows played across the mural of birds and butterflies. The dim light from the fireplace and the candle on her bedside table made it difficult to make out the individual figures. However, as she'd been lying in bed since she'd heard the procession of carriages and baggage carts make its way down the drive, she had most of the mural memorized.

A small part of her wished she'd gone with him. It would not be so terrible to live in London if it meant she might see him every day. Having him in her bed every night might be worth playing the part of the idle duchess, to be trotted out when he needed an ornament on his arm. And to have his child... Even if Endymion became more like his grandfather over the years, she would be there to show her child love, and demonstrate the joy of living life as it came rather than as it was dictated by schedules and rules and the censure of Society over every misstep.

To give her child the life every child deserved, she'd have to fight, and Rhiannon hadn't the heart to fight Endymion. So much of his life had been an act of survival, the most desperate of fights. In the end, that is why she'd refused him. He held her heart, broken as it was. He'd stolen it, and whilst love mended broken hearts, duty and responsibility tended to cause a heart to whither until there was nothing left but contempt, or worse, indifference.

She pulled the banyan she'd pilfered from his luggage from beneath the pillow she'd retrieved from her bedchamber. 'Pitiful' did not begin to describe her actions, but perhaps after all she'd endured these last few days, she was due a bit of the pitiful. Tomorrow, she'd battle Babcock and wrest back control of the estate. Tonight, she'd have a good cry and dream of Endymion in her bed, in her arms, and in her life.

She rolled over and gave the pillow a few punches.

A sudden, loud knock at the chamber door drew her attention.

"Your Grace," Bea called and then flung the door wide. "I'm sorry, Your Grace, but you are needed in the library at once." She bustled into the room and dragged the covers off the bed. "I'll help you to dress."

"Dress? Why do I need to dress to go to the library in the middle of the night?" Rhiannon stumbled from the bed and scooted her feet around in search of her slippers.

Mrs. Davis bustled in with undergarments and a voluminous blue silk dress in her arms. "Get her out of that nightgown. They're waiting."

"They? Who is waiting?" Rhiannon was forced to raise her arms over her head as Bea stripped her of her nightgown and Mrs. Davis replaced the nightgown with a chemise and petticoats and front-closing stays. Bea made quick work of the stays and wiggled them into place to show Rhiannon's bosom to its best advantage.

"This isn't my gown," Rhiannon complained as she fought to settle the yards of silk around her.

"A few well-placed pins and it will be fine," Mrs. Davis assured her. "Miss Smith, do something with her hair."

Rhiannon nearly pinched herself to ensure she was not dreaming, or having a nightmare. Had her maid and housekeeper gone mad?

After a few swipes of the brush and a few well-placed pins, Bea declared, "That will have to do. Come along, Your Grace."

They dragged her out of the bedchamber and down the corridor toward the stairs. Every servant in the household stood in the entrance hall in their nightclothes. What on earth were they about?

"Beatrice Smith, if you don't tell me why I am being dragged to the library in the middle of the night I am going to—"

"Think about it, Your Grace," Mrs. Davis suggested. "It will come to you."

Think on it?

Rhiannon began to drag her feet. She stopped before the library doors where Josiah stood waiting.

"Josiah?"

"Take my arm, lass."

"What is this, Josiah?"

"A chance to make a choice, my girl. For both of you."

"Both? Both who?"

He opened the double doors to reveal Lord Voil and Achilles, dressed in their finest clothes and grinning like fools. Josiah pulled her arm through his and escorted her into the library. A great deal of scuffling, muttering and shoving ensued as the servants crowded in behind her. It was as if she'd been summoned by her governess for an exam for which she had not studied. Then she saw him.

Standing at the far end of the library before the white Italian marble mantel held up by two carved Pendeen dragons stood Endymion, looking nervous and hopeful and...oh Lord, who was that with him? The rector?

"Josiah?" she whispered out of the side of her mouth as they walked slowly across the Persian carpets.

"Say the word and I'll take you back to your chamber and bar the door. But His Grace has gone to a great deal of trouble."

"For what?"

"That, you'll have to ask him yourself. Here we are." Josiah kissed her cheek and placed her hand in Endymion's.

Achilles, dressed in his customary black highwayman garb, stood next to his brother. Lord Voil, dressed in a suit of blue silk breeches, blue silk frock coat, and white shirt with acres of lace at the throat and cuffs swayed slightly on his buckled shoes. Endymion wore similar clothes, save the breeches and frock coat were black. She looked at her own dress and realized she, too, was attired in clothes borrowed from some de Waryn ancestor's wardrobe. The rector, thank goodness, was spared.

It suddenly occurred to her. This rector was the son of the rector who had married her to Endymion seventeen years ago. He was also the boy whose nose Endymion had broken when he'd insulted her. She had the most awful urge to laugh.

"What did you do to convince him to leave his bed in the middle of the night?" she asked her husband under her breath.

"I threatened to break his nose again."

"I thought as much." She patted the rector's open prayer book. "Excuse us for a moment, rector."

"Of course, Your Grace."

She dragged Endymion to the window seat in the corner. "What is this about? Why are you not on your way to London?"

"Is that what you want, Rhee? Do you want me to live in London whilst you live on the other side of England?" He held her hands and ran his forefinger over her wedding band.

"It's what you want. I have no choice in the matter." Her throat began to tighten.

"And if you did? If you had a choice, would you let me stay here in Cornwall? With you?"

"Let you?" she shrieked softly. "I never asked you to leave."

"Why did you do it, Rhee? Why did you strike such a bargain to make me your husband?" He needed to stop looking at her like that, as if she were the only woman in the world.

"Why do you think?" She could not breathe, and it had nothing to do with the tightness of her stays.

"I hope I know, but I want you to say it. Please tell me." He dropped his gaze to her hands once more.

She'd faced angry miners, farmers, murderers and countless other dangers. None so frightening as what she contemplated in this moment.

"I did it because I love you, Dymi. I have loved you since you broke my fall from that tree and cut your thumb. I loved you the night we married, and I love you now. Everything I have done, good and bad, I have done because I love you."

He caught her face between his hands and kissed her. "Thank God for that," he breathed against her lips. "I'd hate to think what you'd do to me if you hated me."

"What is all of this, Dymi? I don't understand."

"Neither of us had a choice, Rhee. Not really. Your father was determined you be a duchess. He would not have let you refuse. Tonight, we have a choice. Will you marry me?"

"Why, Dymi?"

"You've kept my secrets, saved my life, run my estate, and put up with me being a *complete arse*." He touched his forehead to hers. "I married you. I abandoned you. I broke my marriage vows to you, kept my marriage vows to you, and never, ever thought of any other woman more worthy or more desirable to be my duchess. I had no idea why until today. I love you, Rhiannon Harvey de Waryn. Cornwall broke my heart seventeen years ago. This place took everything from me. And you have given it all back. Let me stay here with you. Help me chase away the ghosts. I am the Duke of Pendeen. I am begging you, my love, be my duchess. Marry me. Again."

He gazed at her, his green eyes bright and clear. Here was the boy she'd married. Here was the man she loved. Endymion had made her cry once when they were children. She'd asked his mother what love was because she didn't think love was supposed to hurt. His mother had hugged her tight and smiled.

"Love is a thief, Rhiannon. If you allow a man to steal your heart, rest assured he will break it, and probably more than once. You just make certain the thief is man enough to mend it."

As she stood before the rector in her itchy, borrowed clothes and spoke the vows she now understood with so much more clarity, she realized his mother was right. And no matter the reason all those years ago, Rhiannon had married the only man for her, the only man who could mend her broken heart. And if it took a lifetime, she vowed to be the woman to mend his.

SNEAK PEEK AT A LADY'S BOOK OF LOVE

A LADY'S BOOK OF LOVE

Sir Stirling James, the man Society calls The Marriage Maker, is back this Season to work his magic at uniting couples—and never has his talent been more tested.

Miss Emmaline Peachum needs a hero. She'll settle for a husband, however, if he can rescue her reputation from further scandal and save her beloved library from the bailiff and his henchmen. But what sort of gentleman will agree to marry the daughter of England's most notorious swindler?

After eighteen years in His Majesty's Navy, Captain Lord Arthur Farnsworth wants to retire to the life of a country gentleman. But first, he must discharge his final duty to his men and retrieve the money that was swindled from them.

Sir Stirling James offers the captain the perfect opportunity to find the missing funds. Arthur will marry the bookish hoyden whose father cheated his men of their last farthing and seduce her into telling him where the money can be found.

The problem with this plan lies with the defiant, beautiful, and wickedly witty Miss Emmaline Peachum, who must have inherited her father's larcenous tendencies. While Captain Farnsworth is intent on retribution, she is stealing his heart.

Louisa Cornell

CHAPTER 1

They were staring at her. Not openly, but carefully, so as not to appear rude or ill-mannered. Most ladies found such attentions flattering. Especially when delivered by two handsome and well-dressed gentlemen. Even if the stares occurred in an ancient, rather poorly kept cemetery. Not Miss Emmaline Peachum. She'd had enough attention over the last few months to last Methuselah's lifetime. From barristers. And bailiffs. And Bow Street Runners. And newspapermen. And victims of Reginald Peachum's schemes.

The two gentlemen stood close enough to witness the hurried service, but not close enough to appear a part of it. They spoke to each other—short sentences, sometimes only single words. And still their eyes seldom left her. In her only remaining wool dress, dyed black, and an old bonnet covered in worn black ribbon, she resembled a brown wren in a crow's feathers, and well she knew it. Nothing to attract the intent study of two such lordly specimens.

Emmaline had a peer or two in her family tree, but nothing like these gentlemen. They were both tall and well built, one leaner and taller than the other, but both over six feet. The slightly shorter one was pleasantly handsome. He had a face prone to laughter and good humor. He stood in the graveyard as if at a ball or strolling in Hyde Park. But it was the other who riveted her attention, when she should be heeding the words the rector spoke over her dead father.

The taller man was lean. Hair as black as a starless night sky was as carefully cut as his perfectly tailored clothes. Only when he tilted his head to attend a remark from his companion did she see the long, unruly curls tied in a neat cue at the back of his neck. His face—all slashed angles with sharp cheekbones, a squared cut of a chin, and a blade of a nose. He reminded her of a hawk, a creature of fierce nobility and singular purpose. He was a mast of a man, hewn from some ancient oak, and he stood as if defying any force of God or nature to take him off his feet. Only a sea captain planted himself on solid ground in such a way. His stance and the golden brown of his skin confirmed it—King's Navy through and through. And a captain by the way he tilted his head and studied her. As if she had no business here at all.

She chaffed her hands and clasped them together to hide the holes worn in her gloves. Perhaps it was the cold. Ladies were considered such frail creatures. Gentlemen no doubt considered a London graveyard too dank and chill a place for a lady's delicate constitution. Emmaline could think of no other reason her attendance at her late, not-terribly-lamented father's burial merited such censure. She'd mistakenly assumed no one would attend the funeral of England's latest notorious villain; otherwise, she would not have come. Especially to be delivered a silent scold by two lofty strangers.

That wasn't quite true. Since her brother's death at Trafalgar, Emmaline was the only child her father had left. She didn't want to think of Ned's disapproval had she allowed the man who sired them to go to the hereafter with no one to display at least a semblance of mourning. But then, Ned had escaped their father's schemes and machinations at sixteen, when he ran off to join the King's Navy, only to die in battle three years later. For Emmaline there had been no escape. Until now.

The wind galloped through St. Pancras's graveyard, kicking shards of icy rain against the church's towering stained-glass windows. The patter was almost musical. Which was fortunate, as Emmaline had no money to pay the bell-ringer to toll the death knell. She had no money at all. Everything from the plain wooden casket to the gravediggers had been paid for by the silver-haired rector who now droned out the burial service from the *Book of Common Prayer* with astonishing alacrity for a man of his years. To her surprise, the rector at St. Pancras was a distant relation of her father. Very distant. And very quick to tell her he did not want the relationship known and this last bit of charity was all he had to offer her family.

"Miss Peachum? Miss Peachum?" The rector cleared his throat and gave her an inquiring glance from across the casket waiting to be lowered into the ground. The grave diggers, caps clutched in their hands, looked up with equally questioning eyes. It was cold, spitting rain, and they were ready to be done with it.

Emmaline swallowed painfully and nodded. The men jammed their caps on their heads, took up the ropes slung beneath the casket, and lowered it into the ground. The first clumps of dirt struck the lid. She jumped slightly, with no idea why. Perhaps it was the finality of it all. With the funeral done, her nightmare should be over. Truthfully, it had just begun.

She shivered. Her thin stockings did little to warm the blocks of ice her feet had become. She tugged her last threadbare cloak around her and turned to walk up the stone-paved path toward the front gates of the cemetery.

Only to be confronted by a shouting, gawking crowd of confirmation that all her assumptions about attendance at her father's funeral had been utterly incorrect. She'd not darkened the doors of the Old Bailey a single day of his trial for this very reason. Every newspaperman, scandalmonger, and gawker content to waste his half-day off in London had fought for seats in the courtroom. She'd not have subjected herself to that circus had she wanted to do so. She'd never dreamed her father's funeral would be the same. Then again, she'd never thought he'd die after only a few weeks in prison. Like Ned, he'd made his escape. She was well and truly alone.

How in God's name was she to get home? The cemetery gates nearly groaned at the weight of people pressed against them. The mass of humanity screaming her name stood between her and any chance of finding a hackney, if she had the money for one. She'd not survive trying to fend them off should she attempt to walk to the Sloane Street house from which she'd be evicted any day now. She chewed her lower lip and tapped her foot a beat or two.

"Miss Peachum?"

Emmaline started and turned to find one of the gentlemen who'd studied her. It was the pleasantly handsome one, the one with the open countenance and almost indolent demeanor. His eyes were kind and his voice held the hint of a Scottish burr. He executed a brief, elegant bow.

She stepped back. "Newspaperman, bill collector, or angry gentleman my father swindled?" she challenged with the last bit of confidence she retained.

He smiled. "Marriage maker."

"I beg your pardon?" When had she last eaten? Perhaps a lack of food accounted for this hallucination.

"Allow me to introduce myself. My name is Sir Stirling James and I am aware of your late father's crimes."

"Who in London isn't, sir?" Emmaline wanted only to go home, sit down in her favorite chair—before the bailiff came for it, and enjoy a cup of tea as if her world was not sinking into the seventh level of hell.

"His death has left you without a protector, resources, and soon, no place to lay your head, unless my sources are mistaken."

"Your sources?" She shook her head and made to step around him. Perhaps she might find a hackney or a way home on the other side of the churchyard. "His death ended his troubles, Sir Stirling. His counterfeit lottery tickets and his bilking everyone from a duke's heir to a bawdy house madam was only the beginning of mine." She walked past the other gentleman who'd watched her so carefully from just beyond her father's grave. Something about the way he looked at her sent a shiver down her spine.

Sir Stirling caught her arm and pulled it gently through his own. He patted her gloved hand as it rested in the crook of his elbow. The other gentleman gave her a curt nod and fell into step several paces behind them. She and this Sir Stirling James continued toward the church and then veered around it past the small rectory toward the gates just beyond, where a crested carriage and four stood waiting. A striking black thoroughbred, tied behind, pawed the cobblestones in irritation. The unsettling navy man strode silently to the horse and in one fluid act of grace swung into the saddle.

"Does he speak?" Emmaline nodded in the direction of the horse and rider.

Sir Stirling grinned. "At random intervals."

She shook her head. "I appreciate your gallantry, sir, but I prefer to take care of my own troubles." She tried once more to pull away.

"I may have a solution for your troubles, Miss Peachum, if you are willing to trust me," Sir Stirling said.

"Trust you? In truth we have not even been properly introduced." Emmaline pushed back the brim of her bonnet as he led her to the carriage. A footman lowered the steps and held open the door. "Unless you are a solicitor who has come to tell me I have inherited a fortune from some long, lost relation or a hackney driver who can slip me past that crowd of jackals who are coming this way—"

The navy man brought his horse alongside her.

"I'll handle them."

He spoke! Three words in a rich baritone that seemed to rumble up from an ocean's floor. Or the bowels of hell. Emmaline stared up into eyes the blue grey of an evening mist. A London mist one dared not venture into for fear of becoming lost, body and soul. She felt those eyes on her even after he rode back through the cemetery to head off the crowd that had pushed past St. Pancras's front gates.

Sir Stirling handed her into the carriage and took the seat behind the horses. "If I may be so bold," he started. "You don't need a fortune, Miss Peachum. Your troubles require more drastic measures. You need a husband."

"You need a husband."

Sir Stirling James had said a great deal on the carriage ride from the cemetery to Sloane Street. Emmaline even remembered most of what he'd said. But those four words stood out in her mind and circled her thoughts like the refrain to a child's nursery rhyme. She heard them as he helped her out of the carriage. She heard them as he escorted her to the door of the house her family no longer owned. And she heard them as he took his leave and asked her to consider his proposition.

"What did that one want?" Birdie asked even as she followed Emmaline into the front parlor and divested her of her damp cloak and somewhat bedraggled bonnet. "Money or blood? He's got some cheek dunning a lady at her father's funeral. Even if the father was a conniving thief of the first order."

Trust her faithful maid to get straight to the heart of the

matter. As she was the only servant who remained and had been with Emmaline for twenty of Emmaline's twenty-six years, she had earned the right to be... forthright.

"Neither." Emmaline stepped to the window overlooking the street. The drapes were gone so the view was clear. She sidled behind the wall and peeked around the window frame. Sir Stirling sat in his carriage and conversed with the navy man who had caught up to them on horseback once they turned onto Mount Street. "He wants me to allow him to auction off my hand in marriage."

"Hmpf!" Birdie came to stand beside her. Hands on hips, she made no attempt to hide, but stared blatantly out at the street. "He doesn't look like a cock bawd."

"Birdie!" Emmaline's face blazed with heat. "His name is Sir Stirling James. He's a gentleman."

"Doesn't mean he ain't a cock bawd. Riding in a first-rate carriage, he is. Who's the toff on the horse? His bodyguard?"

Emmaline sidled out of her hiding spot to stand next to her maid. Sir Stirling and his friend, deep in conversation, didn't look back at the house. "I don't know. That one didn't have a great deal to say."

"A man with little to say?" Birdie stepped closer to the window. She shook off Emmaline's restraining arm. "And criminal handsome too. I'd bid on him."

"Who?"

"The man on the horse." She turned to give Emmaline one of her irritating perusals. "You're not dead yet, Miss Em. You'd have to be not to notice a man that fine."

Emmaline snorted. "He has the look of a navy man."

"Happen he knew Mr. Ned. God rest his soul." Birdie rubbed the fog from the windowpanes.

"Let's hope he doesn't find out how many sailors Papa swindled with his lottery."

"Are you going to take the *gentleman* up on his offer?"

Emmaline peered out the window. The Navy man had routed the rabble at the cemetery and caught up with the carriage in short order. Apparently, he was as pointed and quick at command as he was with words.

"Don't be ridiculous," she murmured. "Even if this Sir Stirling could find a gentleman foolish enough to marry Reginald Peachum's daughter, I'm not some prize heifer to be sold at auction. I neither need nor want a husband, thank you very much."

"I don't know about a husband, but even a heifer needs a place out of the rain with winter coming." Birdie fumbled under her skirts and withdrew a key. "The bailiff and his men came by while you were seeing Mr. Peachum put to bed with a shovel. They tried to get into the library, but I told them I didn't have the key." She dropped it into Emmaline's outstretched hand.

"They can't take the books. They're my property, not father's." She started for the parlor door. "I have my grandfather's will and—"

Birdie stayed her with a gentle hand on her arm. "They didn't come to take the books, Miss Em. They came to throw them out into the street so they can prepare the house for the new owners." She took Emmaline's hands and squeezed them gently. "They are coming back by the end of the week."

"So, it is well and truly over." Emmaline looked around the forlorn parlor. She patted Birdie's hand and walked back to the window. Sir Stirling's carriage pulled away. The mysterious gentleman with the intriguing eyes turned his horse in the opposite direction. He looked at the house, into the window, directly at Emmaline. She did not have the power to turn away. He nodded once and set his mount in motion. Her gaze followed him until he turned the corner out of sight.

"Like I said," Birdie said as she joined her at the window. "Criminal handsome." She grinned her wicked Birdie grin. The one she used to cajole Emmaline into a more hopeful mood when all was lost.

"We've had enough of the criminal in this household, Birdie."

"Hmpf! There's criminal and then there's criminal." The maid left the parlor, her merry laughter following her into the foyer and down the corridor to the kitchen.

Their lives were reduced to this. Birdie pretending to be cheerful in spite of their perilous position. Emmaline feigning courage when she had none at all. Sir Stirling and all his talk of making good matches, the sort where love bloomed and the marriage was a happy one. He said he wanted to help her. Marriage had not helped her mother. It had bound her and her children to a criminal. Emmaline would be forced to live with that legacy all her life. Unless...

She dropped her scrunched up shoulders and marched out of the parlor, across the foyer, and down the far corridor to a set of double doors. She fit the key into the lock and opened the doors into the house's small library. With each step she took into the room her anxiety fell and her willingness to consider the ridiculous rose. She pulled the expensive calling card from the pocket of her dress.

No, what she needed wasn't criminal. What she needed was one step above criminal. Sir Stirling James was right. What Emmaline needed was a husband. But on her terms.

CHAPTER 2

"Do I pass muster, sir?"

A gentleman honed many skills in service to His Majesty's Navy. Captain Lord Arthur Farnsworth had not survived eighteen years at sea and come through both Aboukir Bay and Trafalgar with all his limbs intact without an uncanny ability to detect a man taking his measure. Sir Stirling James had been taking Arthur's measure for the better part of the carriage ride to Sloane Street. Unlike French gunners and the occasional fellow officer looking to make a duke's son appear incompetent, the man Society called *The Marriage Maker* had the good grace to admit it when Arthur called him on it.

"You passed muster two days ago, Lord Arthur." The gentleman's Scot's burr was a bit more pronounced today. "Otherwise, we would not be on our way to offer you up to Miss Peachum."

Arthur's lips twitched. "Will the lady wish to inspect my teeth? Or have you done that for her?"

Sir Stirling chuckled. "The lady wasn't interested in your teeth. As I do for any of the ladies for whom I find husbands, I investigated your character, your habits, and your finances. All are without blemish. I would not have allowed you to forego the marriage auction otherwise."

"You informed me the lady is the one who chose to forego the auction. And rightfully so. No woman worth her salt desires to be seen as chattel to be bought and sold."

"Her need is too immediate to wait." Sir Stirling continued to study him, as if looking for some chink in Arthur's carefully crafted façade. "And what of your need, my lord? Why are you so anxious to marry the daughter of a dead swindler, and a highly scandalous one at that? The decision can't sit well with your family."

"She is marrying to preserve her library. To put a roof over her head and her books, if what you have had me agree to on her behalf is true. I should think that as odd a reason to marry as any I might have."

"Perhaps."

"And my family does not know I intend to marry." Arthur fought an urge to swallow. "They have had no say in my life since I reached my majority."

"And became one of the youngest captains in His Majesty's Navy. You are the fourth son of a duke, a wealthy landed gentleman through your own efforts, and an acknowledged war hero."

"I hope you have told my prospective bride all of this. She is certain to accept my proposal." Arthur flicked a speck of dust off his black Weston jacket. "Or perhaps she is clever enough to know what a dead bore it all is."

"I haven't told her anything about you at all. And neither have you." He leaned forward and rested his elbows on his knees. "I will ask you again. Why Miss Peachum?"

Arthur gazed out the carriage window. He had not counted on the man's tenacity. When he'd discovered James's little hobby and his interest in Miss Peachum's plight, Arthur had considered all his options and chosen this as the best way to achieve his aims. The lady needed a husband with a good name to overcome her father's scandal. Before recent events he'd never intended to marry. And once this little charade was over he wouldn't be married. Not really. His promise to his men would be kept and he'd never have to worry about some marriage minded mama throwing her sweet, vapid daughter at him ever again. A wife was a handy thing to have. So long as she was tucked away in the country on one of his smaller estates, out of sight and out of mind. And from what Sir Stirling had told him about Miss Peachum, the arrangement would suit her requirements as well.

"Is it her brother?" the Scotsman asked as the carriage halted before the Sloane Street house.

"Her brother?" Arthur cast about his memory for the information his investigator had discovered of Miss Peachum's late brother. *Edward Peachum. Ran away to sea too long ago to be involved in his father's schemes. Died at Trafalgar.* He suppressed a shudder and took a brief breath to rid his senses of the smell of smoke and blood and the cries of the dying.

He and Sir Stirling disembarked the carriage. A group of burly men milled about on the doorstep of Miss Peachum's house. Something was definitely afoot.

"Lord Arthur." Sir Stirling placed a restraining hand on Arthur's arm. "You would not be the first man to marry a comrade's sister to honor a deathbed vow."

"Do I strike you as the sort of man to marry a woman I have never met for anything less than honorable reasons?" He selected each word as carefully as he might target a ship's hull to force surrender and for much the same reasons.

Sir Stirling studied him. The man smiled—an eerie, portentous smile. The hairs on the back of Arthur's neck rose against the wrap of his neck cloth.

"You are known above all else as an honorable man, Captain Lord Arthur Farnsworth. Indeed," he said as he clapped him on the back and they approached the house. "I am counting on it. Your bride appears in dire need of rescue. Let us go and see if she will allow our help."

~

"DAMN AND BLAST!"

The old musket landed with a clatter on the library table. How was a woman to protect what she loved most with needlework, the pianoforte, or the choice of the proper bonnet when the skill she really needed was how to turn a little round ball and some foul-smelling powder into something useful?

Her grandfather had set store by two things and two things alone—hunting and reading. As such, Emmaline Peachum did not understand why the dear man had not one book in his entire library on how to load a gun. Then again, as his love of hunting was in the tramping about through field and forest from dawn until dusk, it should be no surprise at all. His love of reading was more akin to Emmaline's. He preferred literature, philosophy, and above all, art. A book on how to load a gun was far too practical for a library dedicated to life's finer pursuits.

"I do not have time for this," she muttered as she perused the shelves of books in search of something, anything to aid her cause. Not that she knew the precise time. The clocks had been taken by the bailiff and his men yesterday. A spectacle every resident of Sloane Street had witnessed in a bee swarm of whispers and an entire pantomime of blank stares. Emmaline had not shed a tear, not even when that horrible, red-faced man had come back and snatched Mama's little pocket watch from its place on the drawing room mantel.

She was near to tears now, however, and all for want of a book on how to load a gun. Reginald Peachum would have been more likely to have a book on the subject. Had he considered a book anything more than *a great bloody waste of money*. No, Papa was not one for the written word unless it might be used to swindle his fellow Englishmen out of their hard-earned money. The books covering every shelf in the library had belonged to her grandfather, and they now belonged to her. As did the musket Emmaline had tried to make ready for the last half hour.

One by one she picked up and discarded the array of bits and bobs she'd found in the box with the musket. The musket balls and the odd-shaped pouch of gunpowder made perfect sense to her. If only she might decipher the mystery of how to get them into the gun to make it fire. And fire it she would, if it came to it. She had no choice. She'd never had a choice in life, not really. Until now. And she'd made it.

She'd stood by and watched her home of the last fifteen years stripped bare of every single possession therein. Taken by the bailiff and his men to pay for her father's crimes. The furniture, the paintings, every pot and spoon in the kitchen, even the chamber pots had all been stacked onto carts and hauled away the day her father's trial had ended. They'd come back a few weeks later to take their clothes, her jewelry, the bed linens, and even the rug at the kitchen door. Thank goodness, they'd not thought to look in the cupboard under the stairs, where she'd found her grandfather's gun.

Emmaline had raised neither hand nor voice in answer to these removals. Men had lost their last penny and a few had taken their lives thanks to her father. The sale of the household goods would do little to compensate those he'd wronged. But she'd not begrudge them the few pounds each man might receive once the last vestige of her former life had been put to the gavel.

They would come for the last of it today. And if Sir Stirling James did not show up soon, Emmaline had no choice but to defend the love of her life with an unloaded gun, a viper-tongued maid nigh on to forty, and as much bluff and bluster as she might conjure. Another skill women needed to be taught, to be sure.

"Right, then." Emmaline scrunched her damp eyes with the backs of her hands. She ran her palms down her last clean pinafore and shoved the table a bit closer to the doors. A soft *snick* behind her announced Birdie's quiet entrance from the servant's passage set into the faded, green silk wallpaper at the back of the library.

"Did you manage to load it?" Birdie came to stand beside her and nodded at the musket on the table.

"No." Emmaline sighed. "For all the good it would do us. It would only fire once before they took it away from me. And one member of this family living and dying in the criminal ranks is quite enough."

"So you say, Miss Em." Birdie picked up the musket and handed it to Emmaline. The sound of heavy boot-clad feet scuffing the maid's scrubbed parquet floor rumbled toward the library. "But you don't have to shoot the blighters. Just make them think you will." She crossed her arms and eyed the locked library doors. They shook in their frame against the pounding fists on the other side. "If they think you're a bit mad, per'aps they'll go away and come back tomorrow."

"With the men from Bedlam, no doubt." Emmaline raised the musket and snugged the stock into her shoulder the way her grandfather had shown Ned when they were children. A pang settled beneath her breast. *Ned.* A room of old books and a decrepit musket were all she had left of the fleeting happiness of their childhood together. Loud voices added to the din. Quarreling about the best way to break in and toss her out into the street—books, maid, musket, and all. One final act to the Cheltenham tragedy her life had become. At least the neighbors would be entertained. Again.

"You will cease this harassment at once. The lady and everything remaining in this house are in my charge now."

One voice rose above the others. Not by volume, but by the sheer strength of command in every syllable and word. And there was something disturbingly familiar about that voice. Emmaline and Birdie gawked at each other and then looked back at the doors.

Doors that gave way... with a boom.

Somehow, Emmaline had been knocked flat on her back.

The noise was deafening.

Had they used explosives? All over an on-the-shelf spinster and some books?

Thick smoke permeated the room. Emmaline began to cough. Her shoulder ached like the devil. As did her head where she'd landed on the floor. Her ears rang, but she still heard Birdie's frantic cries.

"Miss Em! Miss Emmaline! Are you hurt?"

She was lifted, none too gently, to her feet. She blinked and realized she held the musket clenched in her hand. She realized because someone was prying her fingers off and handing it to the man standing behind him. *Him*. The man with the dangerous misty grey eyes. All of him was misty now. No. Wait. Smoky. There was a smoking tear in the arm of his jacket. It was a very nice jacket too. The fabric felt expensive. *Felt?* Oh dear. She was clutching his arms for dear life. What had she done?

"I shot you." Well, that was the understatement of the century. The smoke in the room had invaded her head.

"Think nothing of it, Miss Peachum." His lips kicked up on one side. The tall, quiet navy man was smiling at her. Sort of. And speaking to her. Apparently, all it took was a little gunfire. Who knew? "I've been shot at before. Rather used to it actually."

"Then you must learn to keep a better class of company, sir." She sounded mad as a March hare. Emmaline reached for the hole torn in his jacket. He caught her hand and patted it.

"I will take that under advisement, Miss Peachum." He turned to the bailiff and his men. They stood in the corridor and gaped at her. Well out of the line of fire, she noticed. "You men still here? I ordered you to leave. Be about it. Now."

She had never seen such large men leap over each other to leave a place. His voice, so rich and crisp, yet so assured of obedience—Emmaline nearly scarpered out of the room herself. Wait. This was still her house, no matter what he'd said... before she shot him. She stifled a groan.

"Are you in pain, Miss Peachum?"

What? Oh no. Apparently, she *hadn't* stifled that groan completely. And now his eyes bored into hers, half in concern and half in amusement. Amusement? At her. She'd had quite enough of this.

"Who are you, sir? And what is your purpose here?" *Good grief, Emmaline. A little civility wouldn't hurt.* Then again, she'd never shot a man. How *had* she shot him?

"My purpose? Other than serving as a target for your shooting practice?"

"I didn't know the gun was loaded. I couldn't find a book on the subject."

"That is good to know. I should hate to think you ruined my best Weston on purpose."

She heard Birdie snickering none to quietly behind her.

"Who. Are—"

Sir Stirling James stepped around his friend and placed the musket back onto the library table. "Miss Emmaline Peachum, may I make known to you Captain Lord Arthur Farnsworth. As promised, I have found you a husband." The Scotsman was quite handsome when he beamed at her like a benevolent—

What?

Husband?

"Cor', Miss Em. I'll say he has. Can you find me one, sir?"

Emmaline gasped and rounded on her maid with a pointed

glare. Birdie glared back, unrepentant, and nodded at the *criminal handsome* navy man. No, at the captain. She'd been right about him when she saw him in the cemetery. Arthur Farnsworth. Powerful hands, clad in the softest leather gloves, grasped her cold, bare fingers. She had no choice but to turn back and meet his depthless grey gaze. For a moment, a single moment, she allowed herself the luxury, the sheer indulgence of feeling safe, as if one day her life might be ordinary.

"For a gentleman known as *The Marriage Maker*, you are of little account dealing with a lady's sensibilities, Sir Stirling," Captain Farnsworth said, his little promise of a smile tilting his mouth. Still holding her hands, he drew Emmaline to the far end of the library. They stopped next to her grandfather's huge old library globe. The wood of the heavy mahogany stand in which it sat glowed dark red in the light from the morning sun. The drapes in this room had been the first to fall to the bailiff's men.

Where had that thought come from? Emmaline tried to settle her sights on anything and everything save the serenely strong man cradling her hands in his. She failed miserably and finally gave in to the urge to find his face, to search his expression for some clue as to his character. His intentions. Anything about him at all. Birdie was right. It was a crime to be this handsome.

"Miss Peachum." He squeezed her hands. "I know this is all very untoward. I fear your situation is such there is no time for a great many niceties."

Emmaline snorted. "I have not had niceties in my life for quite some time now, Captain. I don't remember them well enough to miss them." She hoped he did not hear the regret in those words.

"Practical. Good." His expression grew solemn, save for those stormy blue-grey eyes. "Still. Miss Emmaline Peachum, will you do me the honor of accepting my hand in marriage?"

Her life to this point raced through her mind, a runaway carriage of schemes, scandal, deaths, all the things she'd been forced to do, and all the ways she was never enough. For her mother. For her father. For society. For herself. And now one more person for whom she'd never be enough invited her to believe she might at least survive. She'd traded so much for the illusion of safety. Was this man simply one more illusion?

"Miss Peachum?"

"I am trying to decide what you are, Captain Farnsworth."

"What I am?"

"A madman? A fiend? I know you aren't a fortune hunter." His mien never wavered. His calm, his way of looking at her made her stomach tighten. Something was falling away from her. She had no idea what.

"A madman? Not enough to draw attention to myself. A fiend? Only to the men who served on my ship. A fortune hunter? Not all fortunes are silver and gold, Miss Peachum."

"Oh." The word left her in a whoosh of air. Her cheeks blazed with heat. "You don't know anything about me, save my father was the most notorious swindler in all of England, and he died in prison. Why would you tie yourself to a name as scandalous as mine?"

"Has she said yes yet, Captain?" Birdie called across the room. Sir Stirling shook with laughter. Emmaline clapped a hand across her eyes and hung her head.

The captain used two fingers to slowly raise her chin. "You are not your name... Emmaline," he said in that dark rumble of a voice. "You are a woman who refused Sir Stirling's marriage auction, because no matter how desperate your circumstances, you still know your worth. That is good enough for me."

Oh, he was good. Truly. He was aloof, and charming, and clever enough to know he'd win her better by flattery and making himself appear harmless. And he was her only hope. Her strength, stretched like antique lace over watered silk, was set to tear and unravel at any moment. She didn't have to trust him to marry him. What a sad testament to a supposedly romantic event.

"Then God help you, Captain Lord Arthur Farnsworth," Emmaline said as she squared her shoulders and tugged her hands from his. "I accept your proposal."

"God help us both," he murmured as she walked back toward Birdie and the mad Scotsman who had set this plan in motion.

www.scarsdalepublishing.com

Made in the USA
Lexington, KY
09 May 2019